THE URBANA FREE LIBRARY
3 1230 00993 0690
W9-AFP-070

Irreversible Things

The Urbana Free Library
DISCARD
To renew: call 217-367-4057
or go to urbanafreelibrary.org
and select My Account
URBANA

Irreversible Things

Lisa Van Orman Hadley

HOWLING
BIRD
PRESS

Winner of the 2019 Howling Bird Press Fiction Prize

© 2019 by Lisa Van Orman Hadley
All rights reserved. Except for brief quotations in critical articles or reviews, no part of this book may be reproduced in any manner without prior written permission from the publisher:

Howling Bird Press
Augsburg University
2211 Riverside Avenue
Minneapolis, MN 55454
612-330-1125

http://engage.augsburg.edu/howlingbird/

Published 2019 by Howling Bird Press
Printed in the United States of America
Book design by Sarah Miner
Cover illustration by Jonny VanOrman
The text of this book is set in Arno Pro.

First Edition

19 20 21 22 23 5 4 3 2

ISBN: 978-0-9961952-5-6

This book is printed on acid-free paper.

For my family:
the one who made me,
the one I made,
and the one I made up.

Table of Contents

PART TWO

Table of Discontents

PARENTS

James, Sr.

Ellen

CHILDREN (FROM OLDEST TO YOUNGEST)

Sara

James, Jr.

Amy

Jonathan

Mark

Lisa

"We look at the world once, in childhood.
The rest is memory."
—Louise Glück

"All art is autobiographical.
The pearl is the oyster's autobiography."
—Federico Fellini

Irreversible Things

Part One

Names

Our last name is Van Orman. It was originally Van Arnhem, after the town in the Netherlands our ancestors came from. Our father has always claimed it means "from the sea," but upon further investigation it appears to mean something like "home of the eagle." We prefer a hybrid of fact and fiction and have decided that it means "home of the seagull."

Every generation has spelled our last name differently—Van Arnhem, VanArnhem, Van Amheim, Van Arnheim, VanOrnum, VanNorman, van Orman, Van Orman. Even now, half our family puts the space in and half our family doesn't.

I put the space in.

The boys all have the same middle name, which is also my mother's maiden name: Ashton.

The girls don't get middle names because we will get married and Van Orman will become our middle names. So someday, the girls will all have the same middle name, too.

Our pets with names are Sparky, Snowball, Frosty, Maui, Sunshine, Peanut Butter, and Pumpkin.

Sara means "little princess." We call her Tairt-Tairt. I don't know where this came from. I think Amy made it up. Tairt-Tairt yells at us every time we call her that.

Jimmy's name is James, like our father, but neither of them goes by James. James means "supplanter" or "take the place of someone due to superior intelligence." Jimmy is the smartest one in the family. His wrestling friends call him Spike.

Amy means "dearly loved," which is very true about her. We call her Amers or Aims. My mother calls her "Amelia Kate," even though her name is not Amelia and, as mentioned, she has no middle name.

Jonathan means "Jesus's gift" or "loyal friend." He goes only by Jonny.

Mark means "fight for truth and righteousness." We call him Marky Tarky, Magoo, or Goo. Later, when we move to Utah, he becomes Thurop, after a sea captain from a movie. People outside our family don't even know his real name.

My name, Lisa, means "consecrated or dedicated to God." When I was born, my parents put my name to a vote: Lisa or Kristen. My brothers and sisters decided which it would be. The most popular name that year was Jennifer. Lisa was the thirteenth most popular. Maybe that's why I always wanted to be a Jennifer. Jonny calls me dork, nerd, baby. Mark calls me buddy. My mother calls me Lou Lou, Leesky Loosky, Weesky Woosky, Sissy. There's a man at church who always calls me "the baby of the family." I hate it. My father calls me "Daddy's baby," which I pretend to hate but actually love. The kids at school call me Lisa Van Mormon. Or Lisa VanMormon. It is always said, never written, so I'm not sure whether there's a space.

We are not allowed to call each other anything with the word *butt* in it, anything with the word *hole* in it, anything with the word *gay* in it, anything with the word *wad* in it, anything with the word *face* in it, anything with the word *head* in it.

My father's name is James Robert, but he goes by Bob. Robert means "bright or shining with fame." Sometimes we call him Fatty McDaddy, which makes him smile and get upset at the same time. My mother calls him Bobby Dear, Sweetheart, Dad. Whenever we ask my mother whether we can do something, she says, "Go ask Dad. His answer is my answer."

Ellen means "torch." My father calls her Ellie Dear. When she was a kid, her cousins called her Ellie the Smelly the Big Fat Belly. Her voice still quivers when she tells us this.

If we ever call my mother a name, my father makes us sit in the bathroom for thirty minutes as punishment. He used to whip the boys with a belt, but he stopped doing that by the time I came around.

When she was a senior in high school, my mother sat with her mother, Mimi, as she lay dying. A few minutes before she died, Mimi called out someone's name. My mother said, "What was that, mother?" and Mimi said, "Oh, I wasn't talking to you, dear."

Every time we leave the house, our parents call after us, "Remember who you are!" which could be another way of saying, "Don't drag our name through the mud!" but which we always take to mean "We love you."

Glossary

gloss · a · ry |ˈgläs-ə-rē|

NOUN

plural *glossaries*

an alphabetical list of terms or words found in or relating to a specific subject, text, or dialect, with explanations; a brief dictionary.

1. The daughter makes a *glossary* of the peculiar things the mother and father say.

gosh |gäSH| **dag · nab · it** |dagnabit|

EXCLAMATION

a euphemism for a widely-used phrase in which a deity is invoked to curse someone to heck, which is another euphemism for a widely-used word representing the devil's fiery realm. This substitution is most often made by those averse to swearing and those strictly observing the Third Commandment. This aversion to curse words may be imposed by one's self, one's religious institution, or one's spouse.

1. When the father misses a serve during a tennis match, he slaps his palm to his forehead and screams, "*Gosh dagnabit,* Bob, you flipping idiot!"

guy · sies |gīzēz|
NOUN
plural of the plural form of *guy*
typically used as a term of endearment to identify or address a group of people with whom the speaker feels particularly close, usually members of one's own family.

1. The family is playing a card game. The mother, out of nowhere, says, "*Guysies,* I like books about little mice."

singular form (rare): *guysie*

2. When all the children have left the nest, the mother turns to the father and says, "Guess it's just you and me, *guysie.*"

heav · ens |ˈhevənz| **to** |to͞o| **Bet · sy** |betsē|
NOUN, PREPOSITION, PROPER NOUN
an exclamation of disapproval or disgust, having nothing to do with an angelic abode or a woman named Betsy.

1. The mother takes the daughter to a movie. When they return to the car after the movie has ended, they discover that they have left the lights on and the engine is dead. The mother nervously calls the father from the payphone in the movie theater to tell him what has happened. He yells, "*Heavens to Betsy,* Ellen! Can't you do anything right?" and then promptly grabs the keys and rushes to the car to rescue them.

woo · ey |wo͞oe|
EXCLAMATION
used to express delight, surprise, or disapproval

1. The mother's parents call to invite the father and the mother to join them on a trip to Egypt. The mother hangs up and remains sitting in the chair saying, "*Wooey! Wooey! Wooey!*" over and over again before she finally gets up to fold the laundry.
2. The mother is in the kitchen doing dishes late at night after the children have been tucked into bed. The father goes around to the backside of the house and lights his face up with a flashlight outside the window where the mother is washing the dishes. The

mother screams, calms down a bit and, resuming her scrubbing, says, "*Wooey*!"

3. The mother is watching a movie with her family. The couple on the screen begins to kiss passionately. The mother squirms in her chair and says, "*Wooey*! They sure don't kiss like they used to. It looks like they're eating each other!"

woo · ey |woōē| **guy · sies** |gīzēz|

EXCLAMATION FOLLOWED BY THE PLURAL OF A PLURAL NOUN

used to express extreme delight, surprise, or disapproval to a group of people with whom the speaker feels extremely close, almost always members of one's own family.

1. The mother comes home, all lit up from a church activity she has just attended.

   She exclaims, "*Wooey guysies,* women love crafts!"

   The daughter challenges her on this, saying, "Mom, you don't even *like* crafts."

   The mother, modifying her statement, says, "*Wooey guysies, most* women love crafts!"
2. The daughter often says "*Wooey guysies*!" in mimicry of the mother. She uses it at first to poke fun at the mother and then, later, because she finds it endearing.

Irreversible Things

JULY 13, 1986. The buzzing has stopped. The cicadas must have gone underground again. When I looked in the *Ci-Cz* volume of the *World Book*, it said that the adults lay their eggs underground and then they die. Their babies will grow up under the azalea bush and then one summer they will come out and leave their skins on the trees and sing their love songs to each other. Then they, too, will die. Like everything else. The next time they come out I'll be twenty years old and I probably won't even live in Florida anymore. I'll be away at college like Sara.

I wonder if Oz will ever come back.

JULY 12, 1986. My mother, Jonny, Mark, and I play Clue. It is my mother's favorite game, but she's sad tonight. The boys and I fight over who gets to be Colonel Mustard. I ask my mother why it's spelled C-O-L-O-N-E-L if it sounds like "kernel"? My mother says she doesn't know.

I am used to my mother knowing everything. It both scares and thrills me that I can ask questions she doesn't know the answers to.

Jonny says I have to be a girl because I'm a girl. I can either be Miss Scarlet, Mrs. Peacock, or Mrs. White. I ask my mother why Miss Scarlet is smoking a long cigarette in the picture on the box and whether she's a bad person. My mother says Miss Scarlet is not a bad person but that she has some bad habits.

I decide to be Miss Scarlet because she is the prettiest.

I put careful "Os" next to the innocent like my mother taught me. I put an "X" next to the person who committed the murder and another one next to the room he did it in and another one next to the object he used.

While we play, Mark uses the cover of the game box to cover up his detective's notes. He is doing something with the pen on the box and after the game I see that he has made a black space between Miss Scarlet's teeth and that he has filled in the whites of her eyes.

I try to take an eraser to the pen so I can make Miss Scarlet pretty again, but it doesn't work. Pieces of her face start rubbing off with the eraser, but the pen stays. The game is ruined forever.

JULY 11, 1986. Amy finds Snowball in the bushes. We bury her next to the marigolds in the garden. We put bowls of food and water out for Frosty. Mrs. Blake next door says we shouldn't let our cat run wild like that. Mrs. Blake is a *mierda* face.

Oz, David, and the twins come over for dinner. This is the first time we've seen them since the funeral. They are living with the Robinsons until things get figured out. I want to tell Oz that I like him, but I am too shy. Instead, I stare into his brown eyes. They remind me of the *cafécito con leche* Mrs. Rojas used to drink from a teacup printed with rosebuds.

Oz tells my mother that dinner is delicious and asks for seconds.

He melts our hearts, my mother's and mine.

He asks if they can come over again soon and I hope.

JULY 10, 1986. I am playing in the front yard when I see a white lump tucked between the azalea bush and the house. I know what it is right when I see it, but I don't go closer. Instead, I run up to my room and lock the door behind me. I crawl under my green and yellow butterfly blanket and cry—for Snowball, for Mrs. Rojas, for irreversible things. I don't tell anyone. I want to bear this secret.

JULY 6, 1986. I go to my first funeral. My father is a pallbearer.

Oz asks Jonny if he knows who killed his mother. Jonny says "your dad" and Oz nods.

I think about Mrs. Rojas standing alone on the front porch at night smoking cigarettes and how different she was from my mother. She had this way of rolling the R at the beginning of Rojas that sounded like a cat purring. I took my shoes off whenever I entered her house. She never told me to—I just had a sense that this was what was supposed to be done. Her house was so clean and the floors sparkled. And it always smelled of coffee. She called it *café* though. She let Oz have a few drops of it in his milk. The coffee turned the milk the same beautiful color of his skin, the same color of Mrs. Rojas's skin.

Mrs. Rojas's casket looks like the cedar chest at the foot of my parents' bed. Sometimes I climb inside the chest and close the lid. The chest smells like mothballs and old fabric and, when I am inside it, I wonder if this is what it feels like to be dead. Then, after a few seconds, I start to worry that I really will die in there and I feel like I can't breathe so I shove the lid open and jump out.

The lid is closed and Mrs. Rojas cannot breathe.

JULY 5, 1986. Snowball is missing. My mother says she probably won't come back. She says sometimes animals find a hiding place to die.

JULY 4, 1986. My mother helps clean Mrs. Rojas's house and helps with the estate sale. She brings home an oak armoire and two matching chairs embroidered with roses. I imagine that the red patterns of roses on the cushions are splatters of her blood. I don't want to touch her things, but I can't stop looking at them.

Frosty immediately claws at the chair cushions and sniffs around the armoire. Then she hops up onto one of the chairs, nuzzles her head under her tail, and takes a nap. Snowball is too weak to jump up so she lies at the foot of Frosty's chair. I help my mother squirt pink medicine into Snowball's mouth to help with the pain.

I play with the twins at the Robinsons' house while my parents go to Mrs. Rojas's wake. Usually I hate playing with the twins because they're younger than me, but everything feels different now. They tell me that they're staying with the Robinsons until their mother comes back. I don't say anything.

We watch fireworks on TV and when we get home my parents let us stay up and light sparklers in the backyard. They say we probably shouldn't play in the front yard for a while, that we should wait until things calm down.

I spell Oz's real name, "Oscar," like his father, in the air with a sparkler in cursive, which I have just learned. The letters glow, suspended in the air, for a few miraculous seconds before they disintegrate into sad, smoky imprints of themselves.

JULY 3, 1986. My father comes home from his trip to Korea. He brings back boxes of white tennis shoes and a pink Minnie Mouse T-shirt. We say thanks and try to smile.

We watch *Liberty Weekend* on ABC. The Statue of Liberty gets a facelift and Neil Diamond sings, "Everywhere around the world, they're coming to America." My mother cries through the whole song.

Oz, David, and the twins go to Disneyworld with the Robinsons. I wonder what happens to you when your father murders your mother. I wonder if we adopt them, can I still marry Oz?

JULY 2, 1986. We read the *News Herald* together. The article says that they found Dr. Rojas in Louisiana. It says they found a pair of his prescription eyeglasses at the crime scene and that he cut his hand when breaking through the living room window. It says that he shot Mrs. Rojas three times as she ran across the street and that she knocked on her neighbor's windows before collapsing on the lawn. Our windows, our lawn. They're talking about our windows and our lawn.

"What are .22-caliber casings?" I ask my mother.

"Gun shells," my mother says.

"What does DOA mean?" I ask.

"Dead on arrival," she says.

"What about a warrant? What's that?" I ask.

"A piece of paper that says a person has to go to jail," my mother says.

"What are quantities of blood?" I ask.

"I don't know," my mother says. "Just blood. Just a lot of blood."

My mother clips the newspaper article to glue into her journal. She stays in her nightgown all day. She lets us watch Nickelodeon and eat cereal for lunch. Jonny and Mark take the newspaper clipping before it can be glued and draw horns on Dr. Rojas and push the points of their pens through his eyes.

JULY 1, 1986. The first thing I always do when I wake up is look for my mother. Today I go into the kitchen first, but she isn't there. I check the living room and study and then I look out the windows. On the side of the house there is yellow tape and lots of policemen and a woman with black hair lying on the grass by the azaleas. I know who the woman is. I run back upstairs to my parents' room.

I find my mother staring out her bedroom window, her right hand heavy against the glass. Her hair is tangled. She wears a light-blue polyester nightgown and she is barefoot, like always. The pads of her feet and the backs of her ankles are thick with yellow calluses. Her bedroom carpet is covered in sewing pins, little landmines waiting to be detonated. I'm always getting them stuck in the bottoms of my feet, but somehow she never does.

Even with her back to me, I know that she is crying. Maybe from the way the hem of her nightgown pulses ever so slightly. She doesn't turn around. She doesn't need to. It is enough to see her moving.

I turn around and go into Sara's old room. Amy sleeps there now since Sara left for college, but I still think of it as Sara's room. Amy is sitting on Sara's old bed. She looks up at me and says, "Mrs. Rojas was shot three times. They think Dr. Rojas did it."

I look out the window. The sky is just beginning to yellow. The male cicadas are buzzing loudly in the pine trees and the females click their wings lovingly in return. Mrs. Rojas is in a black bag now, next to the azaleas. They are so unnaturally pink, like ocean animals or the inside of a stomach. Mrs. Rojas is zipped up inside the bag where there is no air. My mother always tells us to never put a bag on our heads, that it could suffocate us. I want to let Mrs. Rojas out of there.

I wonder what Oz did this morning when he got up and looked for his mother.

JUNE 1986. I hunt for cicada shells on the bushes and trees. They seem to have walked right out of their skins. I peel the papery gold shells off the trees. They are so light and when I hold them up to the sun, I can see right through them.

My father leaves on a business trip to Korea. I ask him to bring me a pink Minnie Mouse T-shirt.

MAY 1986. The cicadas come out of hiding. They crawl up our pine trees and the azalea bush and begin to molt. I check on them every day to see whether they have gotten their wings yet. I peel one off a pine tree while it is still in its shell. I wonder whether it will die now and I try to put it back on the tree, but it won't stay. I drop it to the ground and run into the house, crying. My mother hugs me and asks what's wrong but I can't tell her what I've done.

MARCH 1986. Mrs. Rojas becomes a citizen of the United States. My mother and I wait outside while she takes the test.

Amy is on the Azalea Trail. She wears a dark green plantation dress with matching parasol and sits in somebody else's yard waving demurely as the cars edge along to look at the girls and the azaleas.

Snowball is sick.

JANUARY 1986. Mrs. Rojas wins custody of the children.

It snows. It's only for a few minutes, but Panama City makes those minutes count. The whole town seems to emerge from their two-story houses to dance in the streets and let the tiny white specks turn to water in their palms. People turn on their sprinklers to make ice. School is cancelled. The old man at the end of our street writes, "It snowed here '86" in neon orange spray paint across his driveway.

David, Oz, and the twins play in the snow with us. None of us has ever seen snow before. The snow is different than I imagined it would be. I thought it would be soft like Snowball and Frosty, but the balls are hard and cold. It's hail, really, but we call it snow.

The azalea branches are coated in ice and I wonder whether they will bloom this year. The cats don't like the snow. Even Frosty meows to come in.

SEPTEMBER 1985. Sara leaves for college and Amy takes over her old room. It's lonely sleeping by myself, but at least I have Snowball.

MARCH 1985. We have a party for Oz, David, and the twins. My mother lets me hang streamers and blow up balloons. I help her bake a strawberry cake. She holds her hand over mine and we squeeze the words "Welcome Home!" on the cake together from a tube of red frosting. Jonny and Mark give Oz surf wax and a homemade card. Amy makes a mixtape for David. My mother and I present the twins with new matching Easter dresses my mother sewed for them. She let me pick out the fabric and pattern at the fabric store. When we got home Jonny, Mark, and I wrapped the bolt of cloth around ourselves like mummies.

Oz tells us the story of how his father locked them up in a room in Colombia with no telephone and how they escaped by tying up the maid and jumping from the balcony into their mother's arms.

"Just like Indiana Jones!" I say and Oz looks at me like I'm a *pendeja*. I realize that we know words but we do not know their language.

JANUARY 1985. The house across the street is still empty.

SEPTEMBER 18, 1984. After school, I go with my mother to visit Mrs. Rojas. Besides Mrs. Rojas's lawyer, my mother is the only one who knows where she is hiding. Mrs. Rojas's nose is broken in five places. She and my mother speak in hushed voices about how to get the kids back. They talk about things I don't understand. I wonder when Oz will come home.

SEPTEMBER 17, 1984. It's bedtime and my mother and I are tucked in the bed I share with Amy. She isn't home from work yet. I have my green and yellow butterfly blanket pulled up to my chin and we are reading *Now We Are Six* because I'm almost six. I make her insert my name into all the poems, so instead of, "I think I am a Muffin Man," she says, "I think I am a Muffin Lisa" and instead of "I found a little beetle so that Beetle was his name," she says, "I found a little lisa, so that Lisa was her name." Snowball is curled up on my legs. She always sleeps here. Frosty usually sleeps outside.

In the middle of our reading, there is suddenly a voice in my room saying, "Ellen, it's Aurelia." At first I am scared, and then I remember the intercom. My father put it in when he built our house. There's a speaker on the wall next to my bed. We usually use it to make ghost noises and scare people outside when they are about to ring our doorbell. Last week we scared Jamie Blake so bad he wet his pants and ran home.

I know my mother's first name is Ellen, but I don't know who Aurelia is. It's always strange to hear adults calling each other by their first names. We aren't allowed to call adults by their first names, even if they ask us to. There are certain formalities my mother observes amid her messes, like making the knives face the right way when we set the table and saying, "I'm well," when someone asks, "How are you?" She says addressing adults as Mr. and Mrs. is a sign of respect.

I think the name Aurelia is beautiful.

I follow my mother downstairs and hug her legs as she looks through the peephole and opens the door. Mrs. Rojas is standing in the doorway wearing a nightgown speckled with little pink rosebuds and blood. Mrs. Rojas is Aurelia.

Blood is pouring out of her nose and strands of her black hair are stuck to the blood. Her nose looks wrong. It's crooked and the skin around it is veined and yellow with a deep purple border, like the inside of a plum. I have never seen an adult with bruises before, only children.

My mother puts her hand to her mouth and says, "Aurelia, what's happened to you? Come inside!"

Mrs. Rojas rushes in and my mother shuts and bolts the door behind her. My mother leads Mrs. Rojas into the bathroom and sits her down on the toilet seat. I follow them there, huddled in the doorway. Mrs. Rojas is crying. She says, "Oscar and I got into a fight about who will get custody of the kids. He beat me and then he pushed me down the stairs. And then he took them." It takes me a minute to figure out that she is talking about Oscar the father, Mr. Rojas, not Oz.

My mother twists a washcloth under the faucet and tenderly puts it to Mrs. Rojas's nose. I let the weight of Mrs. Rojas's words seep into me slowly. I never realized that adults could hurt each other, too.

"I'm sure they'll come back soon," my mother says.

"No," Mrs. Rojas says. "No. He said he is taking them back to Colombia. He said if I try to get them he's going to kill me. He poked holes in my tires with a butcher knife."

My mother doesn't say anything for a while and then she says, "I think your nose is broken." She tells me to go back upstairs and she will come back up in a little while to finish reading *Now We Are Six* to me. As I'm walking back up the stairs, I hear Aurelia Rojas say, "I will give up everything, but not my kids. Not my kids."

AUGUST 1984. I hear my mother and Mrs. Rojas talking in hushed voices in the living room. Dr. and Mrs. Rojas are getting a divorce.

1983. Oz teaches us to swear in Spanish. He says that these are the names his parents call each other.

I develop my first crush. I tell Oz he's sexy, a word I heard on TV, and chase him around the yard screaming, "Kiss me, Ozzie, kiss me!"

My mother watches the twins every afternoon while Mrs. Rojas works hanging wallpaper. I don't like to play with the twins because they are babies.

1982. The twins are born. Mrs. Rojas asks my mother if she believes in birth control.

1981. A white cat with no collar shows up at our house. She just walks right through the front door and jumps into my mother's lap. We ask if we can keep her and my mother says we can if we help take care of her. We have a family meeting to decide what to name her. My mother says she looks like the snow with her white fur and we unanimously decide to call her Snowball.

A few months later, Snowball has a litter of kittens. My mother says we can keep one and we have to give the other ones away. We keep the one that looks like Snowball and name her Frosty. Frosty likes to be outside and Snowball likes to be inside. Frosty hisses and runs away when we try to pet her. Every once in a while she follows Snowball into the house and they curl up on the couch together like yin and yang.

1980. We move into the new house on Marywood Drive. The Rojas family lives across the street. David is Amy's age. Oz is a year younger than Jonny and a year older than Mark. I am just a baby. My mother and Mrs. Rojas quickly become friends. My mother teaches Mrs. Rojas how to sew curtains and make casseroles. Mrs. Rojas teaches my mother housekeeping secrets, like how to use vinegar in the dishwasher to get rid of the film on the glasses and on the linoleum floor to cut the grime. My mother is amazed at the difference. She says, "Our kitchen should be on a TV show! BEFORE and *AFTER*!"

1979. My father begins building our new house. My mother plants a bright pink azalea bush on the side of the lot.

Mrs. Rojas, the Colombian woman across the street, drags her hose across the street and waters the bush every day until we are able to move in.

The cicadas are already underground, feeding on the pine and azalea roots, preparing to some day emerge with their love songs and shed their golden skins.

Genesis

We claw ourselves up our mother's body like it belongs to us. We climb into bed with her in the morning, body parts tangled, impossible to decipher limb from limb. We don't know where her body ends and ours begin. We are appendages to her. We ram our heads into her stomach, trying for reentry.

We own a piece of her body. We lived there once so we hold a stake in the real estate. We were born out of her belly button and then the doctor sewed it up. That's why it is puckered and cinched, like a button with four holes sewn so tightly and deeply onto a pillow that it could pop off at any second. It is not a flat, tight spiral like our belly buttons. We know this is how babies come out because when we tell her our theory she doesn't say anything. That means we are right on the money.

We stretch her shirt out, gather the fabric up in our fists and put it in our mouths. We shove our hands into her mouth, slide our fingers along the ridges of her teeth. She pretends to eat us. We grab her pant legs as she walks past us, touch the hem of her garment, try to usurp her power.

When we tickle her we know that, in that moment, we have complete control over her. We are gods.

We lift her shirt and play patty cake with her belly.

"Why is it loose?" we ask. "Is it coming off?"

"It was flat as a pancake before you six came along," she says as she hugs us to her and gives us kisses on our noses.

"And now it's like waffles," we say.

Her body both repulses and beguiles us.

She's bone of our bones, flesh of our flesh, the woman we call Mother. And God took from her a rib and made us.

For Crying Out Loud

Birthdays are special because we get to eat with a special plate and sit at the head of the table in our special hat. We also get to eat special cereal that we don't get to eat the rest of the year. Usually it's Shredded Wheat or Puffed Wheat, but on our birthday we can eat Cookie Crisp or Fruity Pebbles or Peanut Butter Cap'n Crunch. Today all Cap'n Crunches are on sale so my mother says we have to get one of those. That's okay with me though because Fruity Pebbles get soggy too fast and I had Cookie Crisp last year.

I am turning eight and that means I will get baptized on Saturday and confirmed on Sunday. Yesterday we went to the church so I could try on white jumpsuits. They were all too long and too baggy because I am small for my age. My mother says we will roll up the sleeves and pant legs. I want Jimmy to baptize me, but Mom says that Dad's going to do it.

My mother asks what I want for my special birthday dinner.

"Chicken pot pies!" I say, because I love the curly little edges of the crust and the way the filling oozes out of the holes when I poke the top with my fork. I always cut away the edges and save them for last because that's my favorite part.

"Well, let's go see if we can find some on sale," she says.

My mother loves things that are on sale. She'll only buy it if it's on sale or it's a no-name brand. She also clips coupons.

Although we have plenty of money, for some reason she wants us to believe that we're very poor. When we ask for something she always says, "We can't afford that" or "That's too expensive." When I ask if we are rich, she gets a sad, serious look on her face and says, "We're rich in blessings."

The chicken pot pies are not on sale. They're thirty-three cents each. She says, "We can't afford that. That's too expensive."

"But it's my birthday," I say.

"You know what we'll do?" she says, excited now. "We'll make our own chicken pot pies! Homemade is better anyway! And we can do it without the peas. The peas are disgusting. They'll be the best chicken pot pies ever!"

I know the minute she says this that it is a very bad idea. My mother's attempts to make things herself never come out well. I found out about Santa not being real because last Christmas I got a homemade Cabbage Patch doll. What I wanted was a Cabbage Patch doll with a plastic face and red corn-silk hair and a little adoption certificate containing a horrible yet authentic name like Trudy Katrina or Stella Gertrude. I wanted Santa to buy one brand new, right off the shelf, and leave it in the box. I discovered early on that you have to specify this kind of thing for Santa. You don't want Santa left to his own devices in our house.

What I got instead was a Cabbage Patch doll with a fabric face and orange yarn hair. Her clothes were made out of the same fabric my mother used to make Sara's prom dress, which made me suspicious. At first I thought that Santa just didn't like me as much as the other kids who got real Cabbage Patch Dolls for Christmas. But then I got smart and figured it out.

When we get home from Winn Dixie, she gets out the wheat grinder.

"What's that for?" I ask.

"Flour!" she says. "We've got to grind wheat into flour so we can make dough so we can make a crust!"

And now she is taking vegetables from the refrigerator and dicing them into small squares: sweet potatoes (which I hate), mushrooms, carrots, asparagus, and tomatoes. She opens the freezer. There is no chicken left.

"Vegetable pot pies it is," she sighs. I see the resolve crumble from her face for a second, but then it's right back there again and she begins to sing,

Happy birthday, Lisa Lou
I'm making these chicken—
I mean vegetable—
Pot pies for you
Happy birthday, dear Lisa
Happy birthday, Lou Lou

The pot pies are almost done and the smell coming from the oven is nothing like the buttery, chickeny smell of store bought pies. They smell like sweet potatoes and something else, a spice that doesn't belong.

And then I look at the oven and remember something. "Hey, where's the cake?" I ask.

"Cake? Oh dear! I forgot a cake!" my mother says.

"But I wanted a strawberry cake with strawberry frosting," I say.

My father has just gotten home and he peeks his head into the kitchen. "Oh, for crying out loud, Ellen, how could you forget the *cake*?" he says. But then his face breaks into a smile and he pulls a pink box out from behind his back and sets it on the table. It is a grocery store cake with grocery store frosting, new in the box, sealed with tape on the sides and with a little cellophane window on top.

"Strawberry with strawberry frosting," my father says.

Lead

On Valentine's Day, my father brings home bouquets of flowers for the girls. He pulls them from behind his back like a magician—small bunches of pink carnations for Sara, Amy, and I, and a bigger bouquet of red carnations for our mother. The boys get new shoelaces.

When no one else is looking, my father also hands me a brand new mechanical pencil, just like the maroon ones he uses, with an extra tube of .5 lead.

When I am alone in my room, I remove the cap and carefully slip the lead into the pencil—like pointing thread into the eye of a needle, but with much higher stakes.

Myopia

I get my first pair of glasses when I am eight. When I go to school the next day, my teacher, Mrs. Brown, says to the class, "Well now, who is this? Class, it appears that we have a new student!"

A few months later, my vision has already become so blurred I can barely see. I have to take my glasses off and make a little diamond with my thumbs and index fingers to peer through to see the blackboard.

My mother takes me back to the eye doctor. He tests my eyes with my glasses on and then with my glasses off and has me look at the chart of letters that get smaller and smaller.

Then the doctor takes the glasses in his hands, sprays them and wipes them with a cloth with zigzag edges like my mother's pinking shears. He hands them back and I put them on. I can see perfectly.

On the drive home, I am amazed by the things I can see, all the little details.

"Mom, I can see the little *leaves,*" I say. I take my glasses off and put them on again.

"It's a miracle, isn't it?" my mother says.

Lice Day

You never know when lice day is coming. You're sitting at your desk minding your own business and then all of a sudden there they are, marching through the door: the mothers wearing latex gloves and carrying boxes of flimsy plastic combs and stacks of paper towels. I hope it's not my mother. Please, please, please, don't let my mother be a lice lady. You never know when your mother will show up at school. She never tells you she's coming. She drops you off in the morning and then, next thing you know, there she is sitting next to you while they show a movie about how babies are made. Or she shows up to look for lice. But my mother doesn't come through the door today.

The mothers have a list. They start with the As, so I have to wait a long time. Jimmy Anderson. Brooke Avery. Bubba Bennett. Sometimes, if you listen closely, you can hear one of the ladies whisper, "Sue, come look at this." Then the lady named Sue goes over and looks at it and usually shakes her head no. But sometimes she doesn't shake her head. Instead she writes something in her notebook and that kid doesn't show up at school for the next week. Sometimes he never comes back at all. That happened to Daniel Fitzgerald last year.

They call more names and my head starts to itch. It itches so badly, but I can't scratch it. If I scratch it, everyone will think I have lice. So it itches and itches and I bite my lip to keep from scratching.

They're to the T's now. I know there aren't any U's in my class. And then the lady named Sue is saying "Lisa Van Orman." I walk up and sit down in the chair. She takes out a comb and divides my hair into sections. Her hands wiggle around on my scalp. This itches, but I'm not about to say so. Then she begins to comb. She starts at my head and combs down. When she gets to the bottom, she takes the comb and wipes it off onto the paper towel. She looks at the paper towel for a long time. I hold my breath and the itching is out of control.

But she doesn't write anything in her notebook.

Instead, she says, "Steph Winters."

The BBV

The BBV is our Big Blue Van. Our van doesn't have power steering, so when my mother hits a sharp corner, she yells, "Come help me, kids" and we all run up to help her turn the steering wheel. There is a hole in the floor of the car. I like to lie down on the floor while my mother is driving and watch the pavement flashing by. Sometimes little pebbles shoot up and hit me in the face, but I don't care. It feels like a secret world down there that is just for me. The road always looks exactly the same. I am always surprised when I finally get out of the car and see that the outside has changed even though I wasn't looking at it.

Once Amy fell out of the passenger door of the van while we were driving. She cried and cried. We thought it was because she was hurt, but when she finally choked some words out we realized it was because her purse had spilled out onto the pavement and all of her precious makeup was smeared all over the ground, like chalk art.

Carrots

Then: My mother eats so many carrots that her skin turns orange. She eats them while she's driving because she says they help calm her nerves. She eats the stringy skins and the points and she chews the carrots all the way down to their green-brown stubs. The crevice under the van's windshield is packed with sun-bleached carrot stubs.

Then, later: She eats them when she's trying to get down to a hundred pounds. She says sometimes you just need something to keep your mouth busy.

Now: Funny how I always thought my mother was crazy about carrots. I thought they were her favorite food. But she doesn't really keep them in the refrigerator anymore and her skin has more of a bluish tint to it now. When I ask her about it, she says, "Oh, I decided after I turned sixty that I'm only going to eat things I like."

Jesse

The new house my father built is on Marywood Drive. It's in a nice neighborhood full of doctors from South America and the Middle East. We moved out of the old house on Soule Drive when I was just a baby, so I don't remember living there. But I know the old house inside and out because every time someone moves out, we have to clean it.

The old house is across the street from a bayou and there is moss hanging from all the trees. Sometimes Jonny and Mark grab handfuls of the moss and chase me with it, screaming "witches' hair!" I don't really think it's witches' hair, but I run anyway because that moss is crawling with bugs.

The people who just moved out were extra messy. There is garbage everywhere and the house is full of flying cockroaches. The lawn is up to my waist and is growing over the pond in back. Once when I was not being careful, I stepped over the edge and fell into the pond. My father had to pull me out with a two-by-four. The carpet inside the house has to be pulled up because there was a flood the renters didn't tell us about. The house smells like rotten milk and burned grass. Mark finds a pile of *Playboys* in a cupboard and my mother makes a big show of throwing them in the metal trash can outside and lighting them on fire.

I kneel on the lawn to pick weeds with my mother, Amy, and the boys while my father and Jimmy dig out the pond. Sara doesn't have to help because she's working at Sister's Chicken. There are more dandelions than grass and while we pull them up everyone tells stories about things that happened in that house. Mostly things that happened before I was born.

We talk about Mitsuko, our Japanese exchange student, and then about the summer my mother's youngest sister came to stay with us and got so sunburned she had to go to the emergency room.

"Hey, remember Jesse?" Amy asks. "How did you and Dad find him anyway?"

"Oh, that was right after we moved into this house," my mother says. "He was into drugs, he was into pornography, and I think he was addicted to foosball!" She says this last thing about foosball as if it were the worst thing on the list.

"He gambled money on it," she says.

Jesse lived with us before I was born, when my mother was pregnant with Jonny. He showed up at the church where my father was the bishop. He said he was a Mormon and that he needed somewhere to stay. My father called my mother on the phone to see what he should do and she said to bring him home. He was "rough-looking," wearing a T-shirt cut off at the shoulders and a backpack slung over his shoulder.

My mother was always bringing things home. She found injured cats on the side of the road and nursed them back to health. Every Sunday we picked up a wrinkly old woman at the trailer park for church. The woman came home with us after to eat dinner. Her hands shook so badly she could barely get her fork into her mouth. My mother told us stories about her great-grandfather who never turned away anyone who needed help. When someone showed up at his house in need of a meal or bed, he would call to his wife in the kitchen, "Millie, add more water to the soup!" My mother loved this story and wouldn't let us forget it.

Soon after Jesse arrived, things started missing from the house. Things like the real silver flatware my mother got when her mother died. When my mother was polishing the silver, she noticed that a spoon was missing. Then, one day, she looked down at Jesse's hand and saw that he had a silver ring with a familiar rose pattern wrapped around his middle finger. My mother was sure it was the missing spoon.

She confronted Jesse about the ring, but he denied it. My mother was sick about it, but she told herself that the spoon didn't matter. She thought that if she could just give him enough love, that if she could just show him what a normal life was like, that Jesse could change. It didn't occur to her then that he could do anything dangerous.

Then, one day while my father was at work and Sara and Jimmy were at school and Amy was playing at the Alldredge's, my mother opened the door to her bedroom and found Jesse sleeping naked on the queen-sized bed, on top of the good sheets, with my father's rifle resting on his chest.

My mother ran to the gas station and called my father at work. My father met her at the gas station and when they got back to the house, Jesse was gone. They searched the house and discovered that the following things were missing: the rifle, an envelope full of emergency money my parents kept in their closet, and a ring made out of a silver spoon.

My mother sighs and says, "I guess we'll never know what happened to him. Maybe the time he spent with us made a difference. You never know." When we finish picking the weeds, we all move into the house and start wiping out the cupboards. I find little things every now and then. A pack of cards, bobby pins, mouse poop. I don't see why we always have to clean up other people's messes.

Ms. Rear

Ms. Greer has a deep smoker's voice. She's always coughing. Not dainty little dry coughs, but the thick, rumbling kind—like she's erupting. She coughed up tar once in class.

She has a very big backside, so we call her Ms. Rear behind her back.

Ms. Rear keeps a dead cat in a cabinet in the classroom. When she's not in the room, sometimes the boys pull it out of the cabinet and chase the girls with it The other girls run and scream, but I just step back and keep my mouth shut.

She is the worst teacher I've ever had.

When I finally get the courage to raise my hand to answer a question, she scowls at me and tells me to let someone else have a chance for once. The other kids never know the answers.

One day I have to keep going into the bathroom to pull my tights up. She sends a note home with me at the end of the day. When I read it on the bus ride home, it says that I seem to have "bladder problems." I do not deliver the note.

But why I really hate Ms. Rear is because of the Mormon unit. When we get to the Mormons in our history book, Ms. Rear tells the class that Mormons have horns and that they have lots of wives.

I start to shake and raise my hand and say that I am a Mormon and that I don't have horns and that my dad only has one wife. She sends me to the dunce chair for "disrespecting authority." She makes me put a big red cone on my head and sit without saying anything until she tells me I can go back to my seat.

I really hate her.

When I tell my mother about it when I get home, she says "What Would Jesus Do?" and I say Jesus would knock over Ms. Greer's desk.

So my mother makes me sit in the bathroom for half an hour to think about what I've said.

In November, my parents go on a ten-day trip to Egypt and Israel. They leave Sara in charge of all of us. She has her driver's license now.

When they get home, my mother tells us that her luggage was lost on the way there so she wore the same outfit every single day and washed it and hung it up to dry every night. "It was actually really nice," she says, "to not worry about what to wear every day. It was good to live so simply."

They pull out gifts for each of us. Figurines carved from olive wood, polished stones from the Garden of Gethsemane, reproductions of Egyptian papyri. They give me a little velvet box. Inside is a necklace, kind of like a star, but a little different. There are six points with lines on the inside connecting them. After I stare at it for a minute, I see something else: two overlapping triangles, one pointing up and the other pointing down. My mother tells me that it is a Star of David. It is beautiful and was bought just for me and I put it on and resolve never to take it off.

I wear my new necklace to school the next day. Before lunch, Ms. Rear calls me up to her desk. She tells me to give her the necklace. She says I was playing with it and distracting the rest of the class. But I don't remember playing with it. I do remember silently basking in the way the metal felt against my chest, cold and delicate, like a miniature icicle. I unclasp the necklace and hand it over to her. It takes two hands and I fumble around with the clasp. My mother helped me put it on this morning. When I finally get it off, Ms. Rear quickly grabs the necklace from me and tucks it into her desk, as if it is burning hot, a small fire that needs to be smothered.

I know that this is not fair, but I am the child and she is the adult.

I ask her when I can come get the necklace and she says I can come up to her desk after class.

At the end of the day, I go up to her desk. I have been thinking about the necklace all day. I stand in front of her desk for a long time before she looks up and says, "Yes?" She looks at me as though she has no idea why I'm here. I am embarrassed and nervous, but I whisper, "May I have my necklace back? I'm sorry I was playing with it." She opens her desk drawer and rummages around in it for a minute. Then she says, "It seems to be lost now. You shouldn't have been playing with it." I feel the lump coming up my esophagus. The one that rises up in my throat and turns into tears. I turn around before she can see me cry.

I go home and tell my mother what has happened. She tells me she'll talk to my teacher tomorrow. "I'm sure it's still in her desk somewhere" my mother says. "I'm sure she'll find it."

The next day my mother walks into our classroom at the end of class. She stands in the back until the bell rings. She tells me to find Mark and then wait by the flagpole until she comes for us.

We wait for about ten minutes and then she comes walking out with a red face. I can tell she is angry. My mother does not get angry very often. The last time she got red-faced like that was when one of the moms at my soccer game walked up and told her she wasn't a Christian.

When my mom gets to the flagpole, she says, "That is a very difficult woman," and we leave it at that.

Through a Glass

Halloween is on a Sunday this year so our parents make us go trick-or-treating on Saturday night so we don't break the Sabbath. My mother says all the other religious kids will be trick-or-treating today.

Our mother does not believe in store-bought costumes. "Why would you want to look like everyone else?" she says. "Be creative."

Jonny tells me, "Be a nerd. You won't even have to dress up."

I want to be a princess, but when I go up to the attic and dig through the dress-ups, I can't find the right things. So I end up being a nerd.

Jonny, Mark, and I walk to the next neighborhood over, by the church, in our homemade costumes because we are too embarrassed to be seen by the kids in our neighborhood.

We ring our first doorbell and wait. When we're about to walk away, the door opens. A woman in a shiny pink bikini steps out. She has a large white towel wrapped around her head. At first I think it's her costume, but then she looks confused when we shout, "Trick-or-treat!"

"Oh, Halloween's tomorrow, kids!" she says.

"We know," Jonny says, "our mom is making us go today. We're Mormons."

The woman nods knowingly and says, "Well, just a minute, let me see what I can find."

She disappears into the house and comes back several minutes later with a bruised apple, a box of raisins, and a toothbrush. She drops them into our pillowcases and says, "Okay then, have a good night! God bless!"

When she closes the door I hear her say to someone in the background, "Mormons. Poor kids."

At the next house, an old man answers the door. He shouts, "What?" not in a mean way, but as if he didn't hear us. Which he didn't, because we haven't said anything yet. I yell, "Trick-or-treat!" and hold my pillowcase out in front of me and open it as wide as I can.

He squints at my face and I squint back. I'm wearing my father's old glasses with a piece of tape wrapped around the bridge. My father's prescription is very strong and looking through the lenses is like trying to see through a glass of milk.

"You know," the old man says to me, shaking his head, "there are a lot of good optometrists around here. It's a shame to walk around with broken glasses."

"It's my Halloween costume!" I shout, but he doesn't seem to hear me.

"How'd you break your glasses, anyway?" he says.

"They're not broken! It's a costume!" I say.

For the first time, the old man peers at Jonny and Mark behind me. Jonny is dressed like a punk rocker and Mark is a ninja. The old man shakes his head, leans in close to my face and whispers, "You be careful."

"Let's go, nerd," Jonny says. "He doesn't have any candy."

The old man comes out of his house and watches us from his front porch as we walk down his driveway and across the street.

"This blows," Jonny says. "Let's go to the woods."

The woods are across the street from the church. We like to look for things people have left behind in there. The woods don't belong to anyone. They are as much ours as anyone else's. Our parents say we can keep the things we find in there because they are all lost things that people won't come back for. I like to think up stories to go along with the things we find. We find a lot of underwear and shoes with no mates, which I don't touch. Most of the stories I think of for those things do not have happy endings.

When we enter the woods, it is so dark and everything is so blurry through my father's glasses that I have to hold onto Mark's arm to get around. Jonny makes ghost noises and tries to scare me with his flashlight.

Mark says, "Hey, look at this!" and points his flashlight behind a large rock. I lift my father's glasses up for a minute so I can see. There must be twenty or thirty dark bottles nestled back there, covered loosely with leaves. I put the glasses back over my eyes because I like the way familiar things look different with them on.

"It's beer!" Mark says. "I wonder if they're full." He brushes the leaves away and picks up a bottle by the neck. He shakes it. "Hey, they are!"

"Let's smash them," Jonny says.

"Yeah, let's smash them," Mark says.

"I don't know," I say. "I don't want to get in trouble." But another part of me thinks that destroying the bottles is the right thing to do. In church we learned that drinking beer is bad.

Jonny picks a bottle from the pile and cracks it against the rock. It explodes and sprays brown liquid all over us. It fills the woods with a smell that reminds me of the rising loaves of bread my mother makes every Sunday.

I pick up a bottle and my hand starts to shake. I toss it clumsily against the rock but instead of breaking it falls to the ground in one whole piece.

"You have to throw it harder," Jonny says, "like this," and he explodes another bottle on the rock.

I pick the bottle up off the ground and throw it harder this time. It shatters and foam comes spilling out. It feels good. Jonny even pats my shoulder and says, "Good job, nerd."

We destroy bottle after bottle. The broken glass looks like an impressionist painting through my father's lenses. The way the moonlight is hitting it makes it look soft and pixelated and almost holy. The woods smell sweet and musty and the leaves on the ground glisten with the essence of the souls we have just saved.

I see the church steeple across the street as we do it.

We are down to our last few bottles when a pair of headlights comes toward us. A truck pulls up to the edge of the woods. The driver cuts the engine and then a bunch of teenagers tumble out of the truck, laughing. I recognize some of them. They go to school with Jimmy and Amy.

"Run, nerd!" Jonny screams. He and Mark are already far ahead of me. I hear one of the teenagers cuss and then I hear a set of feet crunching leaves behind us, but I'm running faster than I've ever run in my life and I don't want to look back. I think about Lot's wife who looked back at the wicked city and turned into a pillar of salt. My father's glasses fall off at some point, and everything suddenly becomes clearer. I can actually see where I'm going. I don't stop to pick them up, even though the person behind me has stopped running.

When we get home, I run to the top of the stairs and lay down to catch my breath.

After a few minutes we hear a car pull into our driveway and a few seconds after that the doorbell rings.

I watch from the top of the stairs as my mother lets two teenagers, a girl and a boy, into the house. I duck back so they can't see me. The teenagers are angry. They say they are friends with Amy. They tell my mother that we smashed their bottles and they want my mother to give them money. My mother calls for my father. When he comes into the foyer, the discussion becomes heated. My father and the teenagers raise their voices. They talk for a long time.

Then I hear my mother walk down the hall into the kitchen. She comes back with her purse and she takes some bills out. The teenagers take the money and leave.

I stare down those steps.

I wonder why my mother gave them that money.

When my mother comes up the stairs after they leave, she bends down at the top of the stairs and rubs my back. "So how was trick-or treating, Lou Lou?"

"Nobody had any candy for us," I say. "They said Halloween isn't until tomorrow."

"I didn't think about that," she says. "I'm sorry. When I was a kid in Utah and Halloween was on a Sunday, everyone went on Saturday. I guess I thought they would do the same thing here. Sometimes I forget that we're in the mission field."

She doesn't say anything about the beer bottles or the teenagers, but she hands me the pair of my father's glasses that I dropped on the ground when I was running. The teenagers must have returned them to her.

That night when I am kneeling by my bed, I think of the scripture we read in church and the line I love, the beautiful line I underlined with my colored pencil, "For now we see through a glass, darkly."

I think about all that smashed glass shining in the moonlight. And all I can think of is how pretty it looked.

Solo

When I am nine I decide to sing a solo in front of the entire congregation at church. I want to be a solo-singing type of person.

The song is called, "I'm Trying to Be Like Jesus." I memorize all the words and practice the song again and again at home while Amy accompanies on the piano.

When the day for my solo arrives I walk up to the podium with my sheet of music sweaty and shaking in my hands. The bishop brings out a wooden step stool for me to stand on and lowers the microphone in front of my mouth before returning to his folding theater seat behind the podium. The pianist begins to play. I pick up where I am supposed to, my voice trembling but working. I am singing.

I get to the end of the first verse, the part where I am supposed to sing, "At times I am tempted to make a wrong choice/ But I try to listen as the still small voice whispers/ Love one another as Jesus loves you." But something happens and instead I sing, "But I try to listen as he steals my voice." I don't know what to sing after that. I can't think of another word that would make sense. So I stop singing.

The pianist looks up at me, her hands poised above the piano keys, nodding in encouragement, but I just step down from the podium and slide back into the pew with my family.

Jonny and Mark giggle through the rest of the meeting, drawing pictures of my voice being stolen by a thief. But my parents don't say anything. My father puts his arm around me and gives me a squeeze.

When we get home, my mother asks me why I stopped singing.

I shrug and say, "I guess I just didn't feel like singing out loud anymore."

Women's Lib

There was a(n) ________________ woman who lived in a(n) ______________.
ADJECTIVE NOUN (PLACE)

She had so ______________________ ___________________, she didn't
ADJECTIVE DENOTING QUANTITY PLURAL NOUN

__________________ what to ___________________;
VERB (PRESENT TENSE) VERB (PRESENT TENSE)

She gave them some ______________ without any _________________;
NOUN (THING) NOUN (THING)

Then _______________ them all ______________ and put them to
VERB (PAST TENSE) (ADVERB)

________________.
NOUN (THING)

Swing Set

Sometimes when we're bad, my mother goes downstairs and silently exits through the back door. We press our noses against the bathroom window upstairs, the one that looks out on the backyard, watching her. We turn to each other and say, "She must be so mad!" Then we watch, cannot help but watch, as she goes over to the swing set and sits on the black rubber seat.

Her legs never leave the ground, she just pushes herself back and forth, straightening and bending those hourglass legs. And then, maybe it is condensation on the window or maybe something else, but we think we can see tears rolling down her cheeks. When she buries her head in the crook of her arm, it is over. The punishment is complete. The guilt pushes up against our chests, there—right there below the throat and above the collarbone—an almost-choking, almost-ecstatic feeling. Our mother does her time on the swing set and we do our time watching her.

Spike

Jimmy's wrestling friends call him "Spike." I'm not sure why.

He drinks protein powder shakes from the health food store and sometimes he makes a shake for me, too. He says they'll help me get big muscles, like him. I think the shakes taste kind of funny, but I drink them because Jimmy does. They make my stomach feel heavy, like it's full of sand. I cry when I can't get the whole thing down. Sometimes Jimmy makes me sit at the table with my protein shake until I can finish it. The powder is expensive.

When Jonny and Mark fight with me, Jimmy pins them against the floor or the wall until they say they're sorry.

Sometimes Jimmy takes me with him to see his friend Bones. There are no logs in Bones's fireplace, just hundreds and hundreds of cigarette butts. He has black, stringy hair and he's tall and skeletal. I guess that's why he's called Bones. Jimmy and Bones play guitar together and listen to heavy metal. He is in high school with Jimmy, but it seems like he lives alone. I've never seen anyone else at his house. When I open his refrigerator, there is nothing in there except beer and chocolate milk.

Jimmy has an incredibly large neck and veins that stretch through his skin like rodent tunnels. He has very big muscles and he's tan because he's a lifeguard at Shipwreck Island.

He's the only one in the family who can tell my mother to shut up without getting into trouble. At her heaviest, my mother weighs 103 pounds. Twenty-four hours before a wrestling match Jimmy is always exactly 171 pounds. Sometimes he puts her into a headlock, her wrists the size of carrots flailing through the air. She screams, "Jimmy, cut it out! That *hurts*, Jimmy!" Then she screams to us, legs kicking and arms flailing, "Kids, call Dad at work!" And then, only then, does Jimmy finally let go.

He could snap her in a half in a second, but he would never hurt her. He's just joking.

Jimmy is smart. All his teachers at Mosley High School think he's brilliant. He gets straight A's. Sometimes when he's talking, my mother has to run to the dictionary in the office to look up what he's saying.

We have a party for him when he leaves for college. I save up my money from pulling weeds and buy him a canister of protein powder. He's going to BYU—the Mormon school in Utah—where Sara is. My mother says she hopes Jimmy will come back from school different, but I hope he comes back just the same. I don't like people to leave and I don't like them to change. I don't like being the youngest because that means that everyone will eventually leave and I will be all by myself.

We see him off at the airport. His muscles stretch the arms of his short-sleeved shirt and his calves are huge. I run up to him right before he climbs the steps up to the plane. I wrap my arms around the hard circle of his waist and cry.

But he isn't gone too long. He comes home in November. One day he is just living at our house again. I'm so happy he's back, but my mother cries about it all the time.

We don't know why he comes back. Our parents don't tell us anything. Jimmy says he has decided to go to Florida State.

For a while, my mother goes through a lot of days without changing out of her nightgown. She usually plays games with us after school or reads with us until our father gets home. But for a couple of months she lets us watch TV and she spends most of her time bent over the sewing machine or swinging back and forth on the swing set.

A few weeks later, Jimmy is gone. He goes to school in Tallahassee and we don't see him much, even though he's only two hours away.

As for my mother, she finally stops crying and decides to teach a sewing class to girls in the neighborhood. She spends hours finding projects and materials and typing up flyers to be put in mailboxes around the neighborhood.

Possible Reasons Why No One Has Signed Up for My Mother's Sewing Class

1. Girls not interested in sewing.
2. Girls too busy with other activities.
3. Girls out of town.
4. Parents not aware of mother's qualifications as teacher and seamstress.
5. Parents know mother is Mormon.
6. Mothers know how to sew and would rather teach girls themselves.

Puberty in Six Acts

1.

On fifth-grade maturation day my mother walks into the cafeteria and sits quietly beside me on the minty-blue cafeteria bench, the edge of the table digging into our backs. Her tongue moves from side to side along her upper lip like a windshield wiper. This is a habit she has when she is nervous or concentrating very hard, a habit that has recently started to disgust me.

When I left for school this morning, I distinctly remember my mother saying, "See you when you get home." But now, here we are, sitting on this cafeteria bench together watching an outdated movie about Julie's first period.

Julie is a tall, pimpled ballet dancer. She gets her first period in her ballet class at school and her ballet teacher takes her to the library and shows her some books about the birds and the bees. They call Julie's mom and her mother is excited and cheerfully congratulates Julie on entering womanhood. When Julie gets home, her mother has two shopping bags full of different kinds of sanitary napkins and a belt to strap them on with. A belt? And why are they called sanitary napkins, anyway? Shouldn't they be called unsanitary napkins?

My mother leaves maturation day without saying a word to me.

We sit, we watch, she leaves. She doesn't say anything about it when I get home from school that day, either.

I find a book on the bookshelf in the study called *Teaching Your Child about SEX.* The cover shows an adult crouched in front of a young girl with a terrified expression on her face. I read it from cover to cover.

2.

A few weekends later, my mother and I go shopping. When we're in the dressing room trying on clothes, my mother looks at my bare, flat chest and says, "Have you ever thought about getting a bra?"

I say, "yes."

I think this means that we will look for bras next and I start to get excited. The boys in my fifth grade class have started to snap the girls' bras at recess. I am terrified that they will claw at my back and feel that there is nothing there. I *need* a bra.

But then my mother and I don't look at the bras. We walk right past them and my mother doesn't say anything else about it as we leave JCPenney and head out to the ugly blue van.

A few months later, I come home from school and find a Kmart bag at the foot of the stairs containing two training bras—both white with little pink rosebuds in the center. I leave the bag on the stairs and walk up to my room.

My mother knocks on my door a few minutes later. When I open the door, she is holding the bag as far away from her body as possible.

"Lisa," she whispers, "did you see this?"

I say, "yes."

She says, exasperated, "Well, why didn't you bring it upstairs with you before the boys see?"

3.

My eighth grade health teacher, Mr. Bladder, gives us a permission slip for Sex Education that we are supposed to ask our parents to sign. Instead, I take the permission slip home and put it on the Lite-Brite. I go into the kitchen and take the pad of paper from the windowsill where my mother draws little hearts and stars and writes her name over and over again while she's talking on the phone. I slide the notepad under the permission slip and slowly trace the letters of my mother's name through the little illuminated holes of the Lite-Brite.

Mr. Bladder teaches us about different forms of birth control. The one I think sounds the most poetic is the rhythm method, but it turns out that one isn't very effective. He talks about something called a diaphragm, which I always thought had something to do with singing.

I feel like I'm being taught music theory and I don't even own an instrument.

4.

When I finally get my period at fourteen, I don't tell my mother. Even though I knew to expect this, seeing the blood is alarming and I wonder for a minute if I am dying. I teach myself to use tampons because that's all I can find in the bathroom cabinet. I spend hours crouched in the bathroom with the instructions unfolded in front of me, trying all three positions shown on the chart (one leg on toilet seat, standing with legs spread shoulder-width apart, sitting with legs apart) until, as the instructions suggest, I find the position that is the most comfortable for me. I lick my lips in concentration, the way my mother does, until I finally get one in. The minute I get it in, I am terrified that I will get toxic shock syndrome. The instructions say it is a rare but fatal disease. I have six to eight hours to learn how to take the tampon out before things get dangerous.

The first thing I do is go outside to the trampoline to see what happens when I jump and do flips. I remember reading in *Teen Magazine* that you can't even tell the tampon is there, but I can feel it every moment that it is in me. A foreign object, a ticking time bomb. Five hours left.

5.

I do not die.

6.

One day, maybe days later, maybe months, maybe when my mother has reached menopause, the tampons magically appear in my bathroom cabinet, along with a package of pads with wings.

Epistolary Form

Sunday, August 19, 1990

Dear Kids,

We have some exciting news! We will be moving to Utah at the beginning of November. We know this news is probably a surprise to you! We didn't want to say anything until we knew for sure that it was going to happen. Dad has accepted a job at the Air Force base there. We will be sad to leave Panama City, but we know you will love Utah as much as we do. You will make many new friends there. You will also be close to your cousins. Some of my best memories (Mom) as a child were growing up by my cousins. We will also live close to Amy and Sara!

To get ready for the move, we will have a garage sale next Saturday. Please go through your room and find ten things to sell at the garage sale. You will be able to keep the money from the items you sell, so you may want to find some bigger things that you can sell for more money.

We hope you will be as excited about this as we are! We will have a meeting after dinner tonight to discuss ideas for the garage sale and to talk about any questions you have about the move. Please come to the meeting ready to sign up to be on *two* of the following committees:

a. Advertising: responsibilities include making posters for the garage sale and posting them around the neighborhood.
b. Sales: you will be responsible for putting stickers with the prices on the items for the garage sale and collecting the money at the sale.
c. Packing: we will have movers pack up the big things, but you will help pack up some of the more fragile things like china, figurines, etc.

You might want to think about other ways you can help the move go smoothly. You can share your ideas with us tonight. Please meet in the living room at 7:00 sharp!

Love,
Mom and Dad

The Red Tide

Set Up

It is Emily's eleventh birthday party. My eleventh birthday was seven months ago so I am practically twelve.

We get to sleep over by ourselves at one of the condos her parents own. I have been excited all day about watching HBO. I don't even know what is on HBO. I just know that I'm not allowed to watch it.

After her parents leave, we order pizzas. I feel that this is the most adult thing I have ever done. Emily must feel this way, too, because when the delivery guy shows up, she hands him some of the money her parents left in an envelope on the counter and says, "Thank you for your service, young man."

We eat the pizzas on the deck that looks out over the Gulf of Mexico and say, over and over, "Thank you for your service, young man! Thank you for your service!" Emily just laughs and joins in because things like that don't bother her.

The other girls throw their pizza crusts out to the seagulls. I'm a little hesitant because I like the crust, but I don't want to go against the grain (ha!), so I do it anyway. The seagulls seem to appear from nowhere, catching our bread in their beaks the moment it leaves our hands.

While we eat the sky starts to get a heaviness to it, like a gray wool blanket, as it prepares its letdown. I listen to the rolled chord of waves beating out one note at a time on the shore and watch the blue drain out of the water and sky little by little. And all of a sudden, seeing the way the edge of the water grasps at the shore and then recedes seamlessly back into itself, I think about how each moment is gone as soon as it happens. I used to think there was a distinct line between what has happened and what will happen, but now I'm not so sure because I'm already missing these things—the endless ribbon of waves, the smell of rain arriving before the rain, my best friend Emily—even as I'm experiencing them. Knowing that I am leaving and will be doing everything for the last time makes me pay attention to everything like I am seeing it for the first time. And everything looks different.

Even the ocean, usually so clear that I can see the little grains of salt suspended in it, is cloudy and off-color. And the sand, usually white and fine as cake flour, is littered with long knots of seaweed and something that looks like motor-oil.

It's a red tide, an algal bloom, but I don't know that yet. I don't know that there are dinoflagellates blistering beneath the surface, siphoning the oxygen from the water and making it so the fish can't breath. The word *bloom* is so misleading.

The sea is premenstrual, not-quite-red-but-almost. We sit on the deck eating our pizzas and laughing. It's August and I am eleven but I feel on the cusp of twelve.

Playing the Game

"Guys!" Emily says, "I don't know how I'm going to get my contacts out tonight! I learned how to put them in, but I have no idea how to take them out! And I read in *Teen Magazine* that if you sleep with your contacts in, you could go blind!"

Emily got contacts today as part of her birthday present. I'm not allowed to get contacts or get my ears pierced until I'm twelve.

She started wearing glasses even before I did, glasses that looked like two magnifying glasses strapped to her face. They made her green eyes look huge and scientific. You could follow the grains of her irises and see the little flecks of honey-brown in them. When we were little, Emily had to wear a patch over one side of the glasses. The patch was pink and printed with Barbies and I was jealous of it. When I told my mother I wanted one, too, she said that I had to have a lazy eye to get one. She told me that Emily had to wear the patch over her good eye—like benching the best player on the team—and that the lazy one had to exercise all day long.

Now, without the glasses, Emily looks like one of those plain-looking girls from a movie who suddenly takes her glasses off and is drop-dead gorgeous. Her thick gold hair is pulled back into a French braid and her eyes are a monochromatic green. She looks popular. I imagine staying in Florida and becoming a popular girl with Emily, *because* of Emily.

"I better not go to sleep tonight," she says.

When the pizzas are gone we go back inside and turn on HBO and then somebody has the idea to play Truth or Dare, my least favorite game in the world.

I hate Truth or Dare because I don't like to do embarrassing things or tell secrets about myself and because there are no clear rules and no clear winner. Every time I play, every time I have to reveal something about myself or do something I don't want to do, I feel like I've lost—there is a piece of myself out in the world now that can never be recaptured. There was a time when we were playing and I had to tell the name of the boy I liked. Aaron Cantrell. The moment his name left my lips, I didn't like him anymore. Just like that. That's why it is a game I call Losing.

Since it's Emily's birthday, she picks first. She looks around the room slowly, her eyes resting on each girl briefly before moving on to the next. To her left are Emily's school friends, three girls, all named Jennifer. They are tan, polo-shirted, and all have double-pierced ears. One goes by Jen, one goes by Jenny, and one goes by Jennifer. I decide the moment I meet them that I will not learn which is which. And to Emily's left is us—the Mormons—Georgia, Lola, and me.

Georgia's family lives on a swamp and her father wrestles alligators for fun. She's wiry and freckled and her hair is boy-short. She's older than all of us but she seems younger. She comes to church in frilly dresses with skinned knees and real lizards dangling from her ears by their teeth, like earrings.

Lola is the opposite of Georgia. She's big. Not fat, just tall and big-boned. She has wavy blond hair, a big lower lip, and a slight lisp. She looks like a ten-year-old Marilyn Monroe. My mother told me she has juvenile arthritis. I thought only old people could get arthritis, but my mother says hers is different. She gets fevers and rashes a lot because of it. She cried a little after Emily's parents left.

Emily has been my best friend for as long as I can remember. If we were in a play, she would be the actress and I would be the stage crew. I am shy and clever and prefer to work behind the scenes, while she is brave and charming and loves the limelight.

We spend almost every weekend together. Our parents drop us off at each other's houses on Friday after school and then we sleep over until church on Sunday when we go back home with our families.

I like to spend the weekends with her family because her parents take us out for seafood and let me order anything I want from the menu. I order all-you-can-eat fried shrimp and raw oysters every time, even though I always get full after one plate. Her parents don't seem to mind. They tell me to order a drink and dessert. My family hardly ever goes out to eat. When we do, we have to get the cheapest thing on the menu, clean our plates, and only drink water. My father says drinking soda is like "pouring millions and millions of dollars down the drain." Emily's house is quiet and she has a little brother to pick on.

I think Emily likes the chaos of my house. My parents let us do things she's not allowed to do at her house, like sled down our stairs on a twin mattress and ride the zipline my dad rigged from the roof to the pull-up bar in our backyard. One of my father's favorite stories to tell about Emily and me is how he came out into the backyard one Saturday and found us scream-laughing because we had gotten stuck together in a white five-gallon bucket. We were sitting in it, back to back, our legs dangling over either side. The more we tried to wiggle ourselves free, the further down we slid into the bucket until our bums touched the bottom. My father had to cut us out with a saw.

Emily finally chooses one of the Jennifers. I am disappointed and relieved at the same time. Disappointed not to be picked by Emily, but relieved to be able to hold my secrets close for a few more minutes.

The Jennifers all pick each other. It's like the rest of us aren't even there. They all choose "truth" and ask each other questions about people from their school, mostly boys, people I don't know or care about.

The last Jennifer picks Georgia. She doesn't say "Georgia," she just says, "her," looking at Emily and pointing at Georgia.

Georgia chooses "dare," which doesn't surprise me. Georgia isn't afraid of anything.

The Jennifers huddle and whisper and then one of them says, "I dare you to call the Show-N-Tail and apply for a job."

The Show-N-Tail is the local strip joint and prank calling them is our activity, Emily's and mine. We call and pretend we are dancers interested in a job. Because I am the shy one, Emily usually makes the calls while I sit beside her on the bed, telling her what to say next and digging my face into the bed to hide my laughter. How do the Jennifers know about that? The losing has already begun. There's one less thing Emily and I share now.

Emily takes the phone from the bedside table and sets it down next to Georgia. She dials the memorized number slowly with her index finger and then places the phone against Georgia's ear.

"Um, yes, I'm interested in applying for a job." She says it into the phone in a low, sexy voice. "I like to dance," she says, and then she adds "without my shirt on." Her voice is calm as she says all this, a perfect deadpan. All of the other girls are cracking up. After everyone calms down, she returns to the phone and says, "I have big boobies." Georgia does not have big boobies, but I notice tonight that she does have something. Her shirt doesn't quite hang flat over her chest like it used to, like mine still does.

We can hear someone talking on the other end for a long time, Georgia nodding and occasionally saying, "uh-huh" and "okay." Her voice gets a new seriousness to it. Finally Georgia says, "Okay, I will," and hangs up the phone.

"What did they say? What did they say!" we all scream.

"They said for me to come in and fill out an application," she shrugs.

A few years later I will find out that Georgia gets pregnant in high school and runs off into the woods with her redneck boyfriend. And I will imagine her there in the woods making jungle juice in the bathtub, rubbing red berries onto her lips, teaching her daughter how to catch frogs and how to cut the venom out of a water moccasin and roast it over the fire.

Georgia picks Emily. She doesn't even give her the option of truth. She just says, "You have to shave your arms."

It seems like an easy dare, but Emily has the most prolific arm hair I have ever seen. Where I have peach fuzz, Emily has long, billowy arm hairs—so long that they lift and dance in the wind. Once, when we were very small, she came to church and her arms looked like they had a buzz cut. She sat down next to me in Sunday School and whispered in my ear, "I cut my arm's hair with my mamaw's scissors." She said it just like that. *Arm's hair.* I slung my arm over her shoulder and whispered, "Don't worry, they'll grow back."

Everyone follows Emily into the bathroom. She strips down and climbs into the tub. One of the Jennifers has brought a razor and shaving cream. They already shave. Of course they do.

She lathers up, and, with each swipe of the razor, the arm's hair, bundled up in white shaving cream puffs that look like whipped cream, falls off into the bathtub. The shaving cream swirls down the drain, but the hairs do not go with it—the wheat separating from the chaff. They catch on the little holes of the drain, building into a pile and slowing the flow of water until it stops. The bath begins to fill and the hairs lift off with it, circling around Emily, as though they are trying to reattach themselves to her.

When I think of Emily years later, two decades later, I see those gorgeous arm hairs first.

She gets married young, divorced, married again. She has a little girl that looks exactly like her, but without the arm hair. And while I know this is probably genetic, it feels evolutionary, hinged on that moment, adaptive.

There are two people left to pick: Lola and me.

Emily picks me.

Emily knows me better than anyone. She knows that I am terrified of boys, that I have dimples on my bum, that I've never said a swear word. She knows that I get embarrassed easily.

"Dare," I say, finally.

Emily sits there for a long time and then she says, "I dare you to eat that cockroach over there." She points to a cockroach in the corner of the room. It looks dead.

And in this moment, I am grateful. This is doable.

I walk over to the corner of the room and pick up the cockroach. It doesn't move. Its brown body is hard, like armor, and its antennae are long. I close my eyes and plug my nose and raise the cockroach above my mouth. Then, in one quick motion, I put it in my mouth. It makes a sickening crunch between my teeth as I bite down that makes the other girls squeal. The rigid body and wings feel strange and indigestible in my mouth, like walnut shells. But I swallow all the hard pieces, feel the sharp corners against my throat. Then, just like that, it's gone.

"Oh, my gosh, I can't believe you did it!" Emily screams.

She is sitting in front of the TV and we all look over at her at the same time. A naked man and woman are on the screen. They're old—like our parents' ages—and they are doing things I have never seen before. The way they move on the bed, their anatomy, bears no resemblance to life as I know it. The movements are disorienting and mesmerizing and impossible to turn away from. We watch for what seems like hours. Everyone is silent. I get a stomachache.

I feel eleven, early eleven, the farthest possible thing from twelve.

I will look back, years later, and realize the inevitability of this moment. It happens when we turn on HBO. It happens when we are invited to the party. It happens in pieces as Emily and I become—in this order—best friends, inseparable, and then separable. It happens when we are born.

You already know my future.

Ending the Game

There is one girl left to pick: Lola.

"Truth or dare?" I ask.

I figure she'll probably pick truth. I want to go easy on her, to protect her. She told me once that I was her best friend. I knew I was supposed to say it back, but I couldn't. We don't even see each other very often. Mostly at church or when her mother drops her and her little sister off at our house when she can't find a sitter. Lola is sick a lot.

She dies at twenty-nine.

"Double dare," she says, finally.

I don't want to think of one dare for Lola, let alone two.

And then I hear myself saying, "Okay, you have to take your clothes off. And then you have to go out on the deck and scream something."

She looks at me for a long time.

Then she stands up and slides out of her clothes and leaves them in a pile on the floor. Her body does not look like our bodies. She is ten, the youngest of all of us, but her body looks more like the woman's on TV than like ours. But the most shocking thing is her rash. It's bright red and it runs from her collarbone down to her belly button.

We all stare. No one says anything.

And then Lola slides open the glass door and runs out onto the deck. We go out after her. I am surprised that it's beginning to get light outside. I don't know when night passed into day. We didn't even notice it happening. Now the sun is already a half circle above the water. I've always liked the clean feeling of morning, like the whole earth has been laundered overnight, but I realize now that, like Santa Claus, the magic is hinged on sleep. It is morning, but it doesn't feel like morning. I feel dull, suddenly behind-my-eyes tired. I want to go to sleep when it's dark and wake up in the clean of the morning.

The sea is red, not the color of fresh blood but the color the blood makes after it has dried. And then I see all the fish strewn across the sand. There must be thousands of them. I think about how the fish can't live in that water and how they can't live out of it. The seagulls have discovered the fish and are going at them, like birds do. The waves crack like eggs, one by one, their whites running toward shore.

I realize now that the air has a chill to it, as though it has switched from summer to autumn overnight, but Lola seems oblivious to it. She does a full shimmy and in that moment her big, red body seems to be not only shaking, but jubilating. She yells, "Hey, good morning!" to no one but us and all those dead fish and then she runs back into the house again, laughing.

Leaving

Florida

Beach Boys, we say. We want to listen to the Beach Boys.

My mother says she knows the perfect song. She sits cross-legged on the passenger seat because there is nowhere else for her feet to go. The floor in front of her is crammed with all of her books and notebooks and tapes. She shuffles through the shoebox of tapes and finally pulls out the one she's looking for. She puts it into the battery-operated tape player on her lap. The van only has a radio.

My father sighs, mutters "Heavens to Betsy" under his breath.

It's a song called "Salt Lake City!" my mother says.

We know the minute it starts playing that it is not the right song, that it is not the right song at all.

No, not that song, we say. We want a *Florida* song.

We're leaving. The moving truck left yesterday so last night we slept on the floor and ordered pizzas, which my family has never done before. We didn't get it delivered though. I've always wanted a pizza delivered to our house, but it's too expensive because you have to tip the guy, so my father went to pick it up.

Jonny and Mark have their surfboards roped to the top of the van because my father promised to drive them to California to go surfing every month. California will only be twelve hours away.

Yesterday we went to the beach for the last time. The surf was flat so Jonny, Mark, and I ran around in the sand dunes playing a game they made up called headless chickens. On the way home, we stopped at Emily's so I could say goodbye. We didn't say goodbye though. We just got out the Barbies and played with them like we have always done until my mother said it was time to go.

As we're pulling away, April rides past our house on her bike. We've been playing together lately, mostly because my mother tells me that April needs friends. April has asthma. Her mother smokes in the house and when I'm over there, I hold my breath a lot, because of the smoke and because they live by the paper mill, which smells like rotten eggs. There isn't ever anything to eat in April's fridge, just a bunch of beers and empty cartons with flakes of dried milk shaking around in their bottoms. It is a sad refrigerator. My mother says you can tell a lot about people by looking in their refrigerators. Sometimes our refrigerator is so full of food that my dad has to fasten it shut with a bungee cord.

Emily is my best friend, not April. It is Emily I want to see one last time.

But here is April in front of our house, calling my name and waving. As we drive past her, I stick my tongue out. I don't know why I do it and I immediately feel guilty. I don't even know how she got all the way to our house on her bike. It's a really long way.

I will never see her again. That thought makes me feel better and then worse.

My father is in the driver's seat. "We will only stop for gas," he says, "so if you need to go to the bathroom, you'll have to wait until Alabama."

We know, we say. We have done this before. Every other year for as long as I can remember we have driven from Florida to Utah and Idaho to visit our grandparents. Driving nonstop, it takes two days and two nights. This is the first time, though, that we will be doing it for the last time.

My father shows us the map. He has marked the route we will take with a yellow highlighter. I ask him why we can't just go straight there, why we have to go up and then over and then down again. I ask him why we can't just make a straight line from Florida to Utah. He says that we can only go where the roads go.

"But look," I say, pointing at a road I see on the map. "This road doesn't twist and turn. It goes straight."

"It looks like it would be faster, doesn't it?" he says. "But there are things you can't see on maps. Sometimes you just have to learn the roads by driving them. That's probably a dirt road."

I still think my way would be faster.

Alabama

My father hates music so as he drives we listen to talk radio. We listen to a program about how to get lace bugs off the azaleas. We won't have azalea bushes in Utah. We listen to programs about what the Democrats are doing to our country and we listen to the ministry station. After every statement the preacher makes, my father either says, "that's right" or "that's wrong."

"Jesus is our Savior!"

That's right.

"He is God!"

That's wrong.

"The scriptures teach us about God!"

That's right.

"The Bible is the only word of God!"

That's wrong.

"We are saved by grace!"

Well, that's right and wrong, my father says, because we are also saved by works.

Jonny and Mark are sitting in the back seat drawing. I squeeze next to them and watch. I could lean over their shoulders for hours watching them draw. They are playing a game where one of them makes a squiggle on the page and then the other one makes a picture out of it. I wish I could draw what I see in my mind, but words always come instead. My mother says Jonny and Mark take after her mother's side of the family, full of artists. She tells me I take after her father's side. My grandfather used to be the publisher of a newspaper and now he writes inspirational books. I want to be like the artist side.

It's strange with just the three of us. We're leaving Jimmy behind at Florida State. Now we'll only be an hour drive from Sara and Amy in Provo. Sara just got married and Amy's in her first year of college. They thought they were getting away from us, but we're following right behind them.

Jonny tears a piece of paper out of his notebook and hands it to me. "Here, Lisa," he says, "make a squiggle."

Tennessee

Somewhere just outside of Nashville, my mother decides we must go to Graceland.

"Heavens to Betsy, Ellen, it's completely out of the way!" my father says. "It would take four hours to get there and four hours back. It's ridiculous!"

"Bob, I've always wanted to go there and this might be our only chance! Please, Bob."

My parents are both stubborn people. My father is overtly stubborn, but my mother's stubbornness is subtle and absolute. I can tell by her face that if we don't go to Graceland, she will never let my father forget it. He must see this, too, because he sighs and we turn off toward Memphis.

My mother digs around in her shoebox and pulls out her Paul Simon tape. She fast forwards through the first song and then begins to sing along with Paul Simon. Her voice is shaky and off key but she sings with conviction, "For some reason I cannot explain, there's some part of me wants to see Graceland." My mother rolls down the window and puts an arm out, the little hairs on her arm glinting in the sunlight. Her head is turned out so that her hair bobs around in the wind and she sucks the heavy air like a cigarette. Her brown hair looks golden in the sunlight. My mother is golden in this moment. I can smell her lavender soap from this morning, filtering through the breeze, and I wonder what she's thinking of, hanging out the window like that.

During the next four hours, we listen to Graceland over and over. Every time the song ends she stretches out her left hand and presses rewind with her index finger. My father sighs loudly and pops breath mint after breath mint into his mouth.

When we finally get to Graceland, it's closed. My father pulls into the parking lot and cuts the engine. After a couple of minutes, he says, "Well, now you can say you saw Graceland."

We sit in the car and stare at the closed gates. My mother smiles and says, "Thank you, Bob. It was worth it."

And I sense in this moment that somehow it wasn't the getting here that was important. It was so many other things. Something about sunlight and Paul Simon and the smell of lavender soap in November when you're leaving somewhere and going somewhere and you don't know which one is home.

Missouri

Since we stopped in Graceland, my father takes out a pink highlighter and maps out a new course. He tells my mother we will no longer be able to see the Golden Arch. Instead of going through Kentucky and Illinois and then veering left at St. Louis, we will go straight up through the middle of Missouri and over to Nebraska. She looks sad for a minute, but then shrugs and says, "That's okay. We've seen a million golden arches on this trip already!" We never stop at McDonald's though. All our food is in a cooler. McDonald's is too expensive.

My mother drives while my father sleeps on the mattress in the back of the van. We listen to Karen Carpenter, her voice as rich and deep as her sorrow, and then to Andy Williams, which we taped from a record. A song comes on named "Honey" and it makes me cry—not when Honey dies, but when Andy's character finds her crying needlessly in the middle of the day. There is a scratch in the record right there. When I would listen to it at home, I would always lift the needle at just the right moment and then put it back down in the right groove. On this recording, it skips forward. And it will always skip forward now because we sold our records and our record player at the garage sale before we left. That's why I cry.

Sometimes, between tapes, my mother tells us about Utah. She glows with excitement as she talks about a lake that has so much salt in it that it is impossible for your body to sink. She tells us about picking armfuls of yellow and purple wildflowers on the mountain behind her childhood home and the deer that come down and eat the vegetables out of her father's garden. She tells us that we will eat slices of homemade bread as thick as a Bible at the ZCMI mall downtown. She tells us to imagine climbing to the tops of the mountains, like at the end of *The Sound of Music,* and then to imagine seeing the whole city laid out beneath us, the streets fanning out from the temple in neat little rows and the tops of the buildings shining like angelic halos. She tells us the story we have heard a million times, the story of Brigham Young arriving in the Salt Lake Valley with his wagon train of exhausted pioneers, our ancestors among them, and saying, "This is the right place."

Utah is our place. Our people are there. Our history is there. My whole life I've known that I would wind up there eventually; I just didn't know when. The kids at school won't chant "Lisa Van Mormon!" when they see me anymore. I won't have to miss out on Sunday birthday parties and soccer games. I won't have to explain why I'm not allowed to drink Coke. People won't ask me stupid questions like how many wives my father has or whether I have horns. There will be snow. I have only seen snow in the summer when we have come to Utah to visit family—a few hard, almost-melted clumps nestled between rocks at the tops of the mountains. There was that one time it snowed in Panama City, but that doesn't count because it wasn't real snow.

But then I start to think about how there won't be a beach in Utah and how Emily isn't going to be there. I'm going to have to make new friends. I don't know what it's like to have a best friend who isn't named Emily, rocky slopes instead of sand dunes, an accent and way of speaking that reminds me of peaks and ice instead of the slow roll of ocean onto sand.

I am asleep on Mark's shoulder when my mother wakes us up to tell us we're in Kansas City, Missouri. I ask her why it's called Kansas City if it's in Missouri and she says, "Funny, isn't it?" I reach under the seat to pet the dog. He crawled under there as soon as we took off and he hasn't moved since. He bites me. He has never bitten me before.

Nebraska

In Nebraska we stop at Winter Quarters late at night. My father tells us about our ancestor, Elizabeth Hunter Patterson, who came on a boat from Scotland and then crossed the plains to Utah. She stayed at Winter Quarters five years after the first pioneers camped there for the winter, when there were only a few logs and fallen-down cabins left. He says that when she arrived in Utah, she lived in a cave in Red Butte Canyon and gave birth to twins there.

After we leave, I fall asleep and dream of walking barefoot across this land, picking wild berries, sleeping around a fire, and singing songs as I tap the ground with a stick I have found. In my dream, I desperately want to be that pioneer girl in a wild land.

I wake up early. My father is driving and Jonny, Mark, and my mother are asleep on the mattress in the back. There is no music. Just the occasional crescendo and decrescendo of passing semi trucks and the sound of little rocks popping up through the hole in the floor of the van. The sun is just beginning to light up the cornfields. It looks like a painting outside the window with all the farmhouses and the shriveled up cornstalks. I wonder what it would be like to live on a farm. I roll down my window and the cool air surprises me. I think about how a car can take you through seasons. How it can cross that border between worlds, taking you from old to new. I wonder what it will feel like to be so far from the ocean, to be in the middle of things. Suddenly, I miss Emily so much and I feel bad about sticking my tongue out at April. I wonder what kinds of friends I'll get in Utah.

"Beautiful, isn't it?" my father says.

My father and I eat cereal together out of tiny cereal boxes. He has Raisin Bran and I have Sugar Pops. I pour the cereal into little Styrofoam bowls and add milk from a gallon in the cooler. I have become very good at pouring things in the car; I don't spill a drop. My father and I drive forever through corn. He scoots over and lets me sit next to him on the driver's seat and I feel like a little girl again. He smells like breath mints and Old Spice aftershave. He drives fast and my job is to keep my eyes on the radar detector, which he bought especially for this trip. My mother got really mad when she found out about it, so he only brings it out of the glove compartment when she is asleep.

Sometimes he asks me to look at the map and figure out where we are and where we're going next. I trace my finger along the highlighted line, following all the places we've been until I get to the places we haven't been. I learn how to find rivers and lakes and how to tell whether a road is an interstate. I learn how to fold the map the right way, following the direction of the creases.

We don't talk for a long time. We just look out the window together at the long stretch of road ahead of us. Then my father says, "This is the sorriest road I've ever been on. Terrible design. Absolutely terrible. That's because I didn't design this road. In Utah you'll see the roads I designed. Beautiful roads." My father used to design highways. I don't know what he does now, just that he works at the Air Force base. He leaves before I wake up in the morning and comes home at 5:00 with a wet brown bag full of boiled peanuts. He puts the bag on the table just before the bottom gives out. The peanuts taste like ocean and dirt all in one bite.

I will miss the boiled peanuts.

My father says the morning is the best time to work. On weekends, he has already come and gone to the tennis club by the time I wake up, even though I wake up before everyone else. When I wake up and come downstairs, he fixes us both breakfast, he in his tennis whites, I in my pajamas. He puts an ice cube into the bottom of each of our bowls, then granola, then raisin bran, then skim milk, always in that order, and we eat together at the counter. The rest of the family doesn't wake up until hours later, bleary-eyed and cross.

I like to be up with the sun and to go to bed early. My mother says she wishes she were like that. She likes to stay up late writing in her journal and then sleep in as late as we will let her.

After a while, we pull over at a rest stop so my father can use the restroom.

"Where are we?" Mark says sleepily from the mattress in the back of the van.

"I think we're still in Nebraska. We've been in Nebraska for a really long time," I say.

My father comes back out to the car with a can of something in his hand.

"What's that?" I ask when he climbs back into the driver's seat. "Can I have some of that?"

"No," he says. He sets the can down in the cup holder and I can see that it's an RC Cola. Root beer is the only brown drink we're allowed to have.

"Bob," my mother says very quietly and frowns at the can.

"I'm tired," he says. "I need to stay awake. You don't want me falling asleep at the wheel, do you?"

A couple of years ago a man from church fell asleep at the wheel and died.

After we've gone to the bathroom and walked Maui around on the grass to poop, we pile back into the car. But when my father turns the key in the ignition, the car doesn't start.

"Oh, Heavens to Betsy!" he says.

He tries the key several times and then gets out of the car and props up the hood.

"What do you think it is, Bob?" my mother says when he climbs back into the driver's seat.

"I don't know. This would happen out here in the middle of nowhere. For crying out loud!"

"Well, let's say a prayer," she says. "You say it," she tells him.

My father nods and then directs us all to bow our heads and close our eyes and then he says a quick prayer, asking Heavenly Father to start the car.

After the prayer, Jonny asks my father if he can try to start the car. Jonny just got his driver's license. When he turns the ignition, the van starts up, no problem, and we're on our way again.

Wyoming

Somewhere near Cheyenne, a deer runs into the side of our car. Jonny pulls over and we all get out of the van to check out the damage.

"Look at that dent!" my father yells. Next to the dent is a smear of something brown or red, I can't tell which. The deer has limped over into the brush and is laying down now. I start shaking.

"What should we do?" my mom asks. "I just hate to leave that poor deer suffering like this. What do you do in a situation like this?"

"Just look what he's done to our car!" my father says.

"Oh dear," my mother says, or maybe "oh, deer," as we pile back into the van and hit the road again.

Somewhere between Wyoming and Utah, my father says we're on one of his roads. He says it with pride. "It's all about math," he says, "and the angle at which the road curves. You have to get it just right. This is a good road."

Utah

My mother wakes us up when we get to Salt Lake City. She is glowing with excitement. She says it feels good to be home again.

It's dark as we drive up the mountain to Poppy and B's house. Poppy is my mother's father and B is her stepmother. Our house won't be ready for a few more weeks so we're going to stay with them until then. The houses up here are huge—my mother says that one of them even has an elevator. The highest house on the mountain is Poppy and B's house. It's surrounded by scrub oak and quaking aspen. The porch light is on, but all the lights inside are turned off.

I go to open the door to the van, but my mother says, "Wait. We'll sleep out here until morning when Poppy and B wake up. Then we'll go in."

I roll down the window and stick my head out. The crickets are loud up here and the air smells different, like earth instead of salt. The air is cold, but it feels fresher than any air I've ever breathed in my life. It's so thin it almost burns through my nostrils. It travels up my nose and goes all the way up into my head, like sniffing a bottle of rubbing alcohol. I get a nosebleed for the first time in my life and I have to stuff tissue into each nostril to stop the bleeding.

Now the Salt Lake City song, I say. We can listen to it now.

The Many Heads of Roberta Fisk

Roberta Fisk is standing on our doorstep, round and smiling, wearing the most ridiculous purple hat I've ever seen. She kind of wiggles her fingers at me, curtsies, and says, "Cheerio!" in a British accent.

Roberta Fisk is not British. She's schizophrenic and has multiple personalities. When I asked my mother a few years ago what that meant, she said that Roberta hears voices and thinks she is a lot of different people. You never know which person is going to show up. One day she might think she's the queen of England and the next she might think she's a little boy from Boston. She said that Roberta doesn't have any control over it. Then my mother frowned at me and said, "Lisa, there are a lot of people suffering in the world, a lot of people with problems, and we should have compassion for them and help take care of them. That's what Jesus would do."

When I see Roberta on the doorstep, I don't know what Jesus would do, but I know that I want to cry and shut the door in her face.

But I am my mother's daughter, if not Jesus's, so I let her in.

When we moved to Utah seven weeks ago, I thought we would all get a fresh start. I thought that my mother would finally have normal friends, that we wouldn't have to sit next to the stinky people at church, that we wouldn't have to play with kids we didn't like because they needed friends.

But here she is, Roberta Fisk, following us across the country and ruining everything like she always does.

She says she needed a fresh start.

A few years ago, back in Florida, my mother started giving Roberta a ride to church every week. My father was the bishop of our congregation so he had to go to church early on Sundays. This meant my mother had to get the six of us ready and drive us to church by herself. But we never drove to church alone. There was always someone to pick up on the way. The woman at the trailer park who always wore the same stone-washed jean jacket and smelled like rotten apples and smoke. Kids whose parents didn't go to church. The man with shaky hands and deep creases in his face. Roberta Fisk.

When we pulled up in front of Roberta's house, my mother would make whoever was sitting in the passenger seat move to the back.

"But why does *she* get to sit up front?" we would ask.

"Because she's older than you and she's our guest."

We would scowl and make a big show of moving to the back when Roberta got into the car. We resented it because, in our minds, there were certain other things that trumped age. Like sanity. We did not yet understand the mental illnesses lurking in the alleyways of our own DNA.

Roberta lived in a halfway house. I asked my mother what a halfway house was and she said, "A halfway house is for people who have problems. They can't live on their own, but they don't need help all the time either. It's halfway between their old life and their new one. When she gets back on her feet Roberta will be able to live by herself."

Eventually, my mother started taking me to Roberta's on days other than Sundays. "Because she's lonely," my mother said. Roberta would play the Beatles on her record player. She was crazy about the Beatles. She would talk about which of their concerts she had been to, how she owned every single record they had ever released, the meaning behind the song "The Fool on the Hill." I think I saw a glimpse of the real Roberta during those early visits—shy, obsessive, sweet, harmless.

But one day, a few months after we first started going over there, Roberta started saying weird things. She put on a Beatles' record like she always did and then she accused my mother of killing John Lennon. Her face went red and twisted in a way that reminded me of wringing out dishrags over the kitchen sink and then she screamed, pointing at my mother, "I know you killed him! I saw you do it! You killed John Lennon!" She cried real tears. I didn't like Roberta yelling at my mother. It made my head hurt and gave me a stomachache, but my mother just sat there calmly with her hands resting in her lap and didn't say anything until Roberta was finished. Once Roberta calmed down, my mother changed the subject. "Do you think you'll be able to make it to the Relief Society homemaking activity on Wednesday night? We're making just the most darling little things to sell at the bazaar!"

My mother told me on the ride home that Roberta was off her medication.

"Why?" I asked.

"She just stopped taking it. I don't know why."

I didn't understand how there could be a cure for something and that someone wouldn't want to take it.

Roberta cycled in and out of being on her medication. It always took me a little while into our visits to figure out whether she was on it or off it. Her shell was always roughly the same: doughy and pale with greasy hair. It was the inside that morphed. I hated the uncertainty of picking her up and not knowing who was going to be climbing into the car with us. The only person I liked remotely was the first person I had gotten to know—the melancholy, Beatles-obsessed woman who wouldn't hurt anyone.

Before I know it, Roberta Fisk is in our kitchen eating cereal out of a punch bowl and a huge serving spoon. She is telling me, in an American accent now, that because I have blond hair and blue eyes, I am a daughter of Hitler. I am an Aryan. I don't know what that means. I just know that I don't want to be here with her, but I'm the only one home and I don't want to leave Roberta alone in the kitchen. I don't want her to get into our things, to eat our food. And then her voice changes, her whole face changes, and she's saying that she needs to tell me something important. She looks into my eyes and says, "You need to be careful. Your brother Jonny is the spawn of Satan."

I saw a movie once with a woman who has a room full of different heads that have been chopped off other women. She takes one head off and puts on a different one and then she takes on the personality of whoever's head she is wearing. I begin to think of Roberta in this way, as the woman with a room full of heads.

When my mother gets home, I meet her at the door and whisper, "*She's* here."

My mother says, "Who? Who's here?" and I give her a look and say, "Roberta."

My mother frowns a little. It doesn't occur to me until later that maybe when we moved some small part of my mother had wanted to escape Roberta, too.

But then she walks back to the kitchen and says, "Well, hello Roberta! What a great surprise!"

A few weeks later, Roberta disappears. We get a Christmas card from her in December, saying that she got married and she's living somewhere in Idaho. She has changed her name to Ruth. When my mother reads the card, I think I can see a bit of relief in her face. All the little muscles around her mouth and eyes soften.

She puts the card down on the kitchen table and says, "Well, I hope she's doing well. It sounds like she's doing well, doesn't it? She sounds happy, doesn't she?"

A couple of years later my mother and I are shopping at Walmart and we see her at the back of the store. Her hair is cut boy-short and she is with a woman. I'm not sure because she is pretty far away, but I think I see her look straight at us before she slips down an aisle.

My mother and I snake up the aisles until we find her. My mother says, "It's so good to see you, Ruth! It has been ages! How are you?"

"Roberta," she says. "I go by Roberta now."

She seems surprised and sad to see us, like we are the last people she wanted to run into. She doesn't introduce us to the woman she is with.

She seems nervous as she tells my mother that she is very active at church, that she is the visiting teaching coordinator.

On the drive home, my mother says, "Was Roberta acting strange? I mean—did something seem off to you?"

I pause and then say, "Nope. She seemed like herself."

Part Two

Yodeling (Call)

Winter

A few days after I see snowflakes for the first time (unless you count that one time it snowed in Florida), our mother decides we will go skiing as a family. None of us kids has ever been skiing. Our parents haven't been in more than twenty years. They tell us that they each went once before they were married, our father at Sun Valley, our mother at the brand new resort in Park City.

"I never really got the hang of it," our mother says, "but I really think it could be fun to learn now that we're home again."

My mother has always referred to Utah as "our home," even though not a single one of us was born here. Sara, Jimmy, and Amy were born at the military base in Ohio. Jonny, Mark, and I were born in Florida. It never used to bother me, but now that we live here it does. This is not home. Not yet, at least. We've only been here a month.

Leaving Florida felt like being forced to return a book to the library when I was right in the middle of it. Coming to Utah feels like starting a different book halfway through because the first several chapters have been ripped out. At school, everyone talks about things that happened last year—like how the principal got fired for being caught with a prostitute and how Mr. Durfee, everyone's favorite teacher, died. They try to summarize for me, but it's not the same because all the most beautiful and heartbreaking lines get left out. I don't even try to summarize my beginning for them. I will start here, again.

The day before our ski trip, we drive to the Surf and Ski store to get outfitted with boots and skis and poles. I don't understand how it is both a ski shop *and* a surf shop since the nearest ocean is more than seven hundred miles away, but I don't care because the smell of surf wax (branded "Sex Wax"—our mother, as always, is scandalized) immediately makes me feel like I am home again. We toss all our gear on top of the mattress in the back of the Big Blue Van, still there from our cross-country drive.

The next morning we put on turtlenecks and the new coats we bought at the outlet mall the day after we got here. We don't have ski pants, so we wear as many layers of pants as we can fit over one another. I end up in a pair of thermals, two pairs of sweatpants and, on top of it all, a belted pair of my mother's jeans with the words "Gloria Vanderbilt" scrawled across the backside. The last hat left for the taking is an orange one that belongs to my father. It is the color of a construction zone, yelling, "Here I am, watch out!" Which is the last thing I want to scream out to the world. It is a weird hat that goes over my entire face and has two eye-holes that, when I try it on, hit right at my nostrils. I can't see anything but my brothers tell me I look like I have a pig snout.

When we get to the ski resort I realize that this is not what the cool kids are wearing. While they are dressed in coordinated snow pants and parkas with season passes hanging from their zippers, I look like an overweight carpool mom who robs banks on the side. The snow cakes to my jeans and gets inside my socks. My feet burn from the cold as the snow starts to melt, a sensation not too different from the jellyfish stings I used to get every summer in the Gulf of Mexico.

We try the practice hill but my mother is not strong enough to hang onto the tow rope so we decide to just take the lift to the top of the mountain and learn as we go.

I ride the lift up the mountain with my mother. The boys and my father ride together in the chair behind us. My mother says, "Wooey, guysies!"

and "Isn't this magical?" over and over as we rise into the air. All I can think about is falling out of the chair and literally being caught dead in these mom jeans. But then, as we float past the pine trees and it begins to snow right on cue, I have to admit that it *is* kind of magical. The flakes are so light and buoyant and the quiet of the landscape feels so immense and yet so contained that I feel that we must be on the inside of a snow globe.

The snow globe suddenly shatters into a thousand pieces when I look over at all the empty chairs going down the mountain and it finally sinks in: this is going to be a one-way trip. On every other ride I have ever been on, it is nearly impossible to get off once it has started. But the whole *point* of this ride is getting off halfway through.

When we get near the top, my anxiety rising along with our bobbing chair, there is a sign that says, "Lift does not stop. Prepare to exit." I had no idea that the lift wouldn't stop to let us off. Why did no one tell me this?

When we get to the let-off point, I manage to stand up and the chair nudges me forward on my skis. I don't know how to stop so I head up a little slope and then sit down to stop.

And then I look back at my mother. She has fallen out of the chair and is lying on the ground, with her skis crisscrossed in the air. I don't know how to get back to her, so I just stand and watch. The operator stops the lift and helps her up and asks whether she's okay to get down the mountain. Everyone is watching. They tell my mother she can take the tram down if she wants to. She says thank you but she'll be fine. She shuffles over to me on the skis and both of our faces are rosy with embarrassment, or windburn.

When my father and brothers exit the lift, my father guides my mother over to the top of the hill with his arm, and I kind of shuffle-glide on my skis.

"I don't think I can do this," my mother says. "I don't want to slow al
of you down." We all gaze down the mountain together. There is a
immediate drop-off we must face before the run flattens out again.
stand there for a long time, a bunch of beach bums at the top of a mo
tain, with no idea how to get down.

My mother says, "I don't remember ever being this scared."

When we do muster the courage to go down, we all fall almost immediately. But we get up again and after several more falls, everyone starts to get the hang of it, except for our mother. Our father takes her by the elbow and eases her forward, but she just keeps falling down. She finally scoots down the hill on her bottom. When she gets to the section that is level, she says, "I think I'll try cross-country. I think I could be really good at that."

And then she takes her skis off and starts to walk down the mountain. She isn't angry; she doesn't even seem frustrated. She seems relieved. She tells us to go ahead, she'll be fine. "I just want to enjoy the scenery," she says. She tells us to meet her at the lodge at four o'clock. So, we leave her alone. She is good at being alone.

By the end of the first run we are not scared anymore, and by the end of the day we are not falling down anymore.

I am cold and tired and hungry when we meet up again with our mother. She asks us to tell her everything about our day and we do. Then, almost as an afterthought, one of us asks her what she did.

"Oh, I had the most wonderful time!" she says. "I came down here to get something to eat, but everything was so expensive so I just sat down on a bench outside and wrote in my journal. Then the most miraculous thing happened: a man started yodeling on the mountainside. He was dressed in green lederhosen and a little hat with a feather sticking out of it. The sounds that came out of his mouth, well, I have never heard anything like it. When he was done, I told him how beautiful it was and we talked for a while. He works on the tram and sometimes yodels when he is done with his shift. Did you know that yodeling started as a way for alpine villages to call out to one another? It didn't become music until later. I bought one of the tapes he was selling. I'm so happy I didn't buy any lunch or I wouldn't have had any money left over for this!" She waves the tape in front of our faces.

This is so unlike my mother, striking up conversations with strangers. As if in reply to what I am thinking, she says, "I just had a feeling that I should go over and talk to him. I'm so glad I did. This was just the most wonderful day. I can't wait for you to hear this tape."

We listen to the tape on the car ride home. I know this is not what the

cool kids are listening to, speeding down the canyon in their SUVs, but the yodels take hold of me, take hold of all of us, and don't let go the whole ride home. I am amazed at the way one note can go from chest to head, from normal voice to falsetto, and then back again. The notes are both melancholic and joyful, question and answer. They feel like songs I have heard before, or maybe not heard before but that I had known I was going to hear, like all the other sounds in my life had been preparing me for these sounds.

Coming down the mountain toward sea level, I feel caught in the in-between space, mid-yodel, the fraction of a second between what came before and what will come next.

Spring

When it is warm enough and the snow has mostly melted, we hike the mountain behind Poppy's house—Poppy, Jonny, Mark, and me. His is the highest house on the mountain. The deer come down and eat the carrots from his garden. Poppy moved his family up here when it was still wild and uninhabited, before it became a neighborhood for brain surgeons and CEOs. It's the house my mother watched her mother die in.

We leave in the morning, beginning our hike from the front door of his house, each carrying a rolled up plaid-flannel sleeping bag strapped onto an external frame backpack. He calls us his "mountain goats" as we walk up a paved road that turns into a blond dirt road. The road, like an old man, eventually becomes gray and thin; it happens so gradually that we don't even notice until we look down and realize that we are no longer on a road at all, but a trail.

We follow the trail for a long time. "We're hiking!" I think to myself.

But, as it turns out, we are not actually hiking. Nearly an hour in, Poppy turns around and says, "Okay, mountain goats, this is the trailhead. Get ready to hike." I feel duped and my legs already hurt, but I don't say so. Instead, I pretend that I am Heidi, sent to live in the Swiss Alps with a cross grandfather I've never met, determined to win his affection with my cheery disposition and indomitable spirit.

We barely know Poppy. I can't remember him ever coming to visit us in Florida. We drove from Florida to Utah for family reunions every few

disappointing her. I take the T-shirt off in the car when I get to work. Kelly and I get strong and suntanned from hauling bags of dirt and walking customers through buckets of Japanese maples and cherry tree saplings. We sell six-packs of annuals and rose bushes with tightly sealed blossoms. I buy one of the rose bushes for my mother. Its identification tag is ripped off so my boss gives it to me at half price. We don't know what color the blossoms will be. "I always did love a mystery," my mother says as she waters the rose bush.

My favorite section of the nursery is the ground-cover section. From a distance it looks like nothing but packs of weedy dirt, but up close you can see that the containers are teeming with life. The plants remind me of my mother, lying low, often getting stepped on, but swallowing mouthful after mouthful of earth and replacing it with perfect tiny blooms.

After work I stop by the natural food store to buy an apple and a bran muffin, and then I drive up the canyon to hike and think. My mother gets nervous about me hiking alone, so I lie and tell her I was with Kelly. I don't know whether I lie to protect her or myself. Maybe both.

At the beginning of the summer, I think I will do a new hike every day, but then I give up and hike Poppy's mountain again and again. I see deer, an occasional elk and, once, a moose. My legs become muscled. I was hoping they would get skinny, but they don't. If anything, my calves and thighs become even more pronounced. The inner thighs of my jeans become distressed. I have my mother's hips and thighs. All of us girls do. She always apologized to us about them, saying, "I'm sorry you got my thunder thighs and child-rearing hips, girls."

I inherited Poppy's waxy-covered book of wildflowers. Poppy put a blue asterisk next to all the wildflowers he saw up here. I add my own asterisks next to his. My list is growing: cinquefoils, dog's-tooth violets (not actually violet, but yellow), Indian paintbrush, columbine. I look for new flowers, but the mountain is dry and colorless this summer. We are in a drought.

I think of how green it was that first spring with Poppy.

He died two summers ago. We hiked with him one last time a couple of months before he died. He was slow that year. When we got to the meadow, he stopped and told us to go ahead. He sat down on the grass to wait for us. It was the first time we had summited without him. We got home so late that our mother was waiting anxiously in her nightgown on the front steps. She had called the police.

Poppy ran two miles the morning he died. He came home from his run, had a stroke, and died in the hospital that night. He is the only person I have ever watched die. The nurse told us we could tell when he was gone by watching the lines on the monitor, but I watched him instead. When the nurse told us he was dead, there was no sign that he had passed. He looked exactly the same in the moments before he died as he did in the moments after, and it made me think that maybe death isn't a moment, but a series of moments. Maybe you *become* dead, slowly, like a small hole in an air mattress that releases air so gradually that you don't notice you are sinking, until you are lying on the hard ground. Maybe death is like that.

When I am not in the mountains, I use them to orient myself. As I drive around Salt Lake City, I can tell which direction I am going by the position of the mountains. The familiar mountains, the one I hiked with Poppy and the one our family skied on when we moved out here, are to the east. The foreign mountains are to the west. I have never been to those mountains, even though they are only a forty-five minute drive across the valley.

I remember driving around in Florida with my mom in the Big Blue Van. We were constantly getting lost. She was always saying, "I get so turned around here. It's just trees and sky everywhere and they all look the same. In Utah I always knew where I was because of the mountains."

It's true, too. Her sense of direction is spot-on here. It makes me wonder whether some people really have a bad sense of direction or whether they just haven't found their right place yet, their center.

On one hike, so hot and dry I can't sweat, it hits me that I am the same age my mother was when her mother died. My mother was a senior in high school. I never really understood until now how early that is to lose your mother, and I am suddenly choked with panic at the thought of losing her.

My mother constantly compares herself to her mother. It is her way of orienting herself in the world.

When we were kids, she would say, “My mother never yelled at us,” right after she had yelled at us.

“My mother never said an unkind word about anyone,” after she said made a comment about someone that was less than glowing.

My mother will never measure up because she never got to see the mistakes her mother would have made.

One morning I look out my window and see that the rosebush in the backyard has bloomed the most gorgeous pink orange color.

Halfway through the summer Kelly tells me she will not be going to Hawaii with me. She has decided to go to a college in Southern Utah. I have not applied anywhere else. I assumed she hadn’t either. Hawaii was my only plan.

I ask my mother something I have been thinking about lately. I say, “Did you decide not to go to Hawaii because your mom died?”

She says, “Yes.”

I say, “Why didn’t you say that when I asked you the first time?”

And she says, “I didn’t want to take that moment away from you.”

At the end of August, when the backyard smells like grapes and the petals are dropping off my mother’s rosebush, my parents see me off at the airport. I am excited, ready for adventure. For the first time in my life I board a plane alone.

When I step off my flight, I am hit first with the humidity and then with the smell of flowers. I don’t know what kind of blooms they are, but I always did love a mystery.

Fall

When the other students ask me where I am from, I don’t know what to say. Am I from Florida or Utah? When we moved to Utah, it was easy. I was from the place I lived before. I was not from there. But now what?

Am I only from the place I lived before this or the place I lived before that, too? Am I from the place where I spent my childhood or the place where I reached adulthood? Will I add Hawaii to the list once I leave?

I usually say, "Well, I was born in Florida but I've lived in Utah for the last six years." I can see in their faces that this complicated answer registers as nowhere.

The campus is circular with single-story classrooms that have direct entrance from the outside. I study the plants as I walk from class to class. They are so different from any plants I've seen before. The blades of grass are fat and coarse against my bare feet. The pine trees are strange, too. The needles are soft and thick and the branches look like upside-down palm fronds. The palm trees remind me of Florida. Except for the rats that run up and down them. The feral cats outside my dorm window are always chasing them in the middle of the night. Their mewing is low and pitchy, nothing like our cats at home.

I wonder whether there are annuals here? If winter never comes, how do the plants know when to die?

My roommate is from Hong Kong and she goes out every night with all the other students from Hong Kong. They give each other American names. My roommate's name is Agnes. Her Chinese name is Kam Fung. Her best friends are Stella and Ernestine. She asks me whether the names they have chosen for each other are cool. I tell her that they are not cool, but that they are unique which is much better than being cool. This seems to be a good answer. One night I come home and Agnes has a crockpot full of sweet red beans and dumplings on her desk. I ask her if I can taste some. She says I probably won't like it as she ladles it into a Styrofoam bowl, but she is wrong. I love it. She serves me bowl after bowl and watches in delight as I eat. She tells me I should have been born in Hong Kong. Then she tells me I am getting fat. I think of how I could reinvent myself here. I could be anyone, from anywhere. I could be a fat girl from Hong Kong.

I befriend a student in my dorm from Indonesia named Fatima. This is her first time in the United States, but she seems more American than me. She is in love with American pop music. She doesn't understand how I don't know the words to the songs she is singing. "But it's a top hit here!" she says. "I'm sorry, I just don't listen to that music," I say. She asks what I listen to, so one day I hand her my headphones. When she takes them off, she says, "Oh, that's sad. Why do you listen to that?" She wants me to teach her all the slang. She always gets it a little wrong. She says, "That is so suck!" and "This is so junk!" and "Hello, America!" I adore her.

I make another friend in the dorm named Hanim. She tells me that in Turkish her name means "Mrs." It's an appendage to a name, a limb without a body. She has lived in Turkey her whole life but her parents are expats. She tells me that she went to American schools in Turkey and had mostly American friends.

During the week, I spend so much time in the air-conditioned library that I wonder why I came all the way to paradise for school. The college doesn't turn out to be great. I know this because I am at the top of my math class. I have never been anywhere near the top of any math class I have been in.

On Saturdays, Hanim, Fatima, and I go hiking together in the mountains in the morning and then we go to the beach in the afternoon, and on these days I know that I could not be anywhere else but here. I fall in love with the jagged cliffs that reach down toward the sea—cliffs that started under the ocean and then pushed their way up so that part of them is under the water, and part of them is above it. I do not have to choose between mountains and ocean here.

I can have both, like a yodel, going back and forth between low and high, joy and melancholy, between longing for where I was, and where I want to be.

Winter

There are no seasons here except rainy and not-as-rainy, bigger surf and smaller surf. When I call home on the pay phone in the courtyard of my dorm, my mother asks whether I miss the winter, meaning the snow. I tell her that, honestly, I don't. Maybe it's because I was born in a place without snow (unless you count that one time).

What I don't say is how much I miss her. It is a physical ache, somewhere between my stomach and my head. I remember how, when I was a kid, I used to wish that I were a kangaroo so I could climb in and out of her pouch. What I really wanted was to escape my world for a moment to return to the place I came from.

I don't care what she says. I just need to hear her voice.

"Oh, but I love the seasons," she says, "I always missed them when we lived in Florida."

I guess the first place you live stays with you and calls out to everywhere else you go, asking for a response.

Nodes

My mother calls me one day and casually tells me that they have found something in her lymph nodes.

"What are lymph nodes?" I ask, humbled that my mother still knows things I don't.

"Little things in your armpit."

"Okay," I say. "But what does that mean?"

She tells me they're going to do a biopsy to see if it's breast cancer, but that it's probably benign. Benign: kind. I learned that word in my middle school English class. I don't remember ever hearing it in the real world until now. It's not used the way I thought it would be.

But did she say breast cancer? Her mother died of breast cancer.

I demand that she call me as soon as she finds out the results of the test.

Two weeks later, someone comes to my room and tells me there is a call for me on the pay phone. I answer the phone, jittery like on Christmas morning, but nothing like that.

"I have something to tell you," my mother says, after we have said our hellos.

I can't speak.

"My Aunt Judith died." Aunt Judith who brought me lemonade when I worked at the plant nursery. She was a lovely woman.

"But what about the biopsy?" I say.

"Oh, that came back fine," she says. "Benign."

The Wig

My grandmother's hair is on the dresser, balancing on top of a can of All Weather Aqua Net hairspray. The hair does what the can says it will: it extra super holds. The hair is the color of a seagull—white and gray with a little bit of black showing underneath. The strands, like feathers, all move in the same direction and tuck under one another perfectly.

My grandmother's hair has taken flight.

I look over at the bed where my grandmother is asleep under the sheets and then scan the rest of the room, searching for clues. It's like looking at one of those pictures in *Highlights Magazine* where you have to find what's wrong—the page that always gives me a stomachache that I can't stop looking at. A boy waterskiing on the sidewalk. A girl with a pepperoni for a hand. A woman wearing a snorkel in the middle of the desert. A grandmother's hair across the room from the grandmother. I wish I could flip to the back of the magazine and make this picture right.

I have seen wigs before. Our dress-ups box is full of them. The wigs are matted and impossible to sink a brush into. I like to put them on and pretend to be someone else for awhile. Or a different version of me. I am always relieved when I take the wig off and I look like myself again. But in that split second after taking the wig off my head, I see myself in my entirety, all the pieces coming together to form a whole, the way a

I don't know whether I did it or not.

When I think about that day now, as an adult, I always remember standing there staring at the hair on the Aqua Net can and then looking over at the shape of my grandmother under the sheets, but I never remember what happened after that. It's strange to me now that what seems to be the most important part of that story is missing. But I cannot recall it. I have memories of pulling back the sheets and memories of not doing it and all the details contradict one another.

For example, I'm sure my grandparents were visiting our house in Florida and going into their room at night was a mistake. I woke up in the middle of the night and meant to crawl into bed with my parents—I had forgotten that they were sleeping on the couch downstairs and that my grandparents were sleeping in their bed. Seeing the hair on the dresser was not only alarming in the sense that it was disconnected from my grandmother, it was also alarming because my grandmother herself wasn't supposed to be in that room.

But I feel equally strongly that it had to have been my grandparents' house in Idaho. It was mid-afternoon and my grandmother and grandfather were taking a nap in their room. I went into their room because my grandmother had promised to take us to the junk store.

I wonder if all these things can be true at the same time.

Sometimes searching through my memory feels like incorrectly reading one of those Choose Your Own Adventure books I loved when I was a kid—reading it from cover to cover instead of flipping forward and backward to the proper pages. What I remember is a simultaneity of possible outcomes instead of a sequence of actual events.

If I decide to look, turn to page 103.
If I decide not to look, turn to page 104.

stranger might see another stranger. I am new. Then familiarity sets in and the moment is gone.

My grandmother sometimes wears a light blue turban on her head when she's working around the house. The turban always seemed too small to be able to fit the poof of her hair. I figured it was some kind of optical illusion, a little trick my grandmother had up her sleeve, like when she showed me how eyeliner can make your eyes look bigger, or how you can tell how healthy you are by looking at the moons and ridges of your fingernails. Sometimes she lets me play dress up with the turban and I pin an old brooch onto its center and pretend I'm the wizard from *The Wizard of Oz*. Now that I think about it, I have never seen her put it on or take it off.

I walk slowly over to her bedside. I hear the rhythm of her breath, steady as a metronome. I want to pull back the covers and find out what story lies between the sheets.

Everyone tells me I look like my Grandma Van Orman. I don't see it because I have only known her old. It is hard to think backward about how someone would have looked many years ago. It is easier to put on wrinkles than take them away.

As I stand over my grandmother, ready to pull back the sheets, I feel like I am about to see into my own future.

I peel back the covers slowly, just enough to see her head. She is completely bald. Well, no, that's not true. Not completely. Her head is covered in soft down, like a baby's. I only look for a moment before my grandmother wakes up, angry, and tells me to go back to bed. She pulls the covers back up over her head and I run back to my room, terrified.

The next morning I wake up early and go downstairs. My grandfather is at the table. The newspaper is spread over his lap and he has a mug of coffee nestled between his hands. The coffee is our little secret. Mormons aren't supposed to drink coffee. He gets up when he sees me and pours me a bowl of raisin bran with half-and-half. I love half-and-half. I only get to have it when I'm with my grandparents. They put it on everything. They don't even buy milk.

I sit down at the table and pick out the raisins with my spoon and put them in a little pile next to my bowl, like I do every morning. Jonny and Mark are always saying, "Why don't you just eat just eat bran flakes, you weirdo?" Bran flakes just taste different, flat. It's hard to explain.

"Grandpa, how come you're bald?" I ask.

"Grass doesn't grow on a busy street, Lisa. Hair today, gone tomorrow."

I wonder whether he knows something, whether Grandma told him about what I have done. But he doesn't say anything. We just keep eating our raisin bran. I realize what it is: I like the taste of the raisins *having been there.*

Turn to page 105.

I stand over the bed, hear my grandmother's breathing, and I can't do it. I can't look. I walk away from the truth.

My whole life I wonder what she looks like under there. I have nightmares about pulling the wig off her head, only to find another, and another, and another, and another. An endless head of wigs.

Whenever we stay with her in Idaho, I watch from the garden level window as she waters the flowers each morning in her wig, plaid shirt and polyester slacks. She bends over the peonies, those tight fists of petals closed in on themselves like miniature cabbages, until I cannot see her face anymore. I wonder what she's thinking about, what secrets she is hiding. Her head dips so low I don't know how the wig stays on her head. I begin to wonder whether it isn't her real hair after all. Maybe I made up the story of the hair on the dresser.

I make up stories about her. She is a spy and she wears the wig as a disguise so no one will know her true identity. She lost her hair to a disease. She is not-quite-human, an electric grandmother, like the one I read about once in a book.

I kick myself for not having looked when I had the chance. But at the same time I worry that once you pull back the petals, you've ruined the flower.

Turn to page 106.

I see the wig on the dresser again, much later, as she lay dying. I sit beside the bed in her condo and watch over her as she hallucinates and sleeps. The wig is perched on a featureless Styrofoam head, next to the light blue turban and prescription bottles. The hair still holds its shape. It looks gigantic now. I guess it was always that big, but it looks even more exaggerated now in comparison to her.

My grandmother's face is creased and hollow. Her body is tiny. She isn't eating well. Her hands are cold when I hold them.

As I watch her sleep, I think about how little I know of this woman laid out before me. My relationship to her was always defined by what she did for me. It was a give-and-take relationship where she did all the giving and I did all the taking. She was always getting down games or finding crafts for me to make when I was bored, taking me to the junk store or to the IGA grocery, and then ducking into her apron to prepare the next meal. The only thing I know about her past is that she grew up Methodist and became a Mormon when she met my grandfather. And that she was a Democrat. I remember the way my parents said "Democrat," like it was something to forgive her for because she didn't know better.

I take the wig off its perch and arrange it on her head as she sleeps. I don't even look at her real hair.

I want her to look like she has always looked. To feel the way I felt before I knew she wore a wig. I need to close the curtain. I need an illusion.

Turn to page 107.

I see the wig on the dresser again, much later, as she lay dying. I sit beside the bed in her condo and watch over her as she hallucinates and sleeps. Her hair is perched on a Styrofoam head, the scary, featureless kind you see in a wig shop, next to the light blue turban and prescription bottles.

The wig looks exactly the same after all these years. But it looks huge now in comparison to my grandmother. She has gotten smaller. The skin on her face is collapsing in on itself. She isn't eating well. Her hands are cold when I hold them.

When I look at her head, the buzzing curiosity I felt as a child is gone. The hair is white and wavy, not thick, but enough. It has a soft wildness to it, untouched by decades of hairspray. But there is something alarmingly artificial about it, too. All those years I watched her, watering her peonies, canning salsa in her kitchen, reading the moons of my fingernails, and the whole time she was wearing the wig. The wig had become a part of her.

I am left to wonder, which one is her true hair? Maybe something was never wrong with the picture. Maybe this was always the right one.

I go over to the wig and remove it from its perch. I put it on my head and shift it around until I think I've found the front. It smells like generations past, stale and sweet, the smell of objects outliving their owners.

I model the wig in front of the mirror on the dresser and am startled at the resemblance.

When I finally take it off and put it back on the dresser, I am surprised at what I look like. I study the stranger in the mirror until she slips away and I turn back into myself again.

Turn to page 107.

After she dies, my father brings home a box of her things. I am surprised to find the wig at the bottom of the box. I had always assumed she would be buried in it. The wig smells like her and I feel closer to my grandmother than I have in a long time.

I ask if I can have the wig and my father gives it to me.

I want to ask my father now to tell me the story of why she wore the wig and what all of it means. Except my father can't tell me. His mind is a trap door. The story may fall out from beneath us at any moment. I should have asked him years ago.

I ask my mother what she knows about it, but get very little. She says, "I don't know. I think she didn't like her hair or she had psoriasis or something." Maybe she just wanted to look like someone else. Or a different version of herself.

Her hair is layered.

Every story is a choose-your-own-adventure.

Now, the gray mass is perched on top of an old roller skate in my closet, still stiff with Grandma's Extra Super Hold hairspray. Sometimes I get the chills when I open the closet and see it sitting there with no head filling it.

Slipping

"Okay, now where's the car parked?" my father asks for the fourth or fifth time.

"We took the train in, remember Dad?" I say for the fourth or fifth time.

"Oh, that's right!" he says, shaking his head, but I can tell he doesn't remember.

When we get back on the train, my mother and I sit across from my father.

"Lisa," my mother says, too loudly, "Have you noticed that Dad's memory isn't as sharp as it used to be?"

"Yes," I whisper, stealing glances at my father to make sure he isn't listening. It seems like a betrayal to talk about him this way, right in front of him. But he appears not to hear us. He's staring out the window, squinting at the blank panels and harsh lights of the underground.

The truth is, I haven't seen my dad in almost a year and his personality has changed so much that I hardly recognize him. My father—the engineer, the church leader, the woodworker, the jokester, the quick-tempered patriarch of our family—he's slipping.

"Over the last year, he's really gone downhill," my mother says. "He gets really mixed up sometimes, and his short-term memory is getting really bad. It scares me. I always thought he'd live longer than me. He has such good genes."

Good genes. When I was a kid, I always thought people were saying, "He has such good jeans."

I look out the window just as the train pulls out of the underground and over the Charles. It's dark and the stars are beautiful tonight, as they so rarely are in the city. They fill the sky in a way that makes it seem like there are more stars than sky and it makes me wonder for a second which one is containing the other. I look down and see the stars in the water, watch them stretch and contract in the ripples like a funhouse mirror.

I think of my father's memory and the way it contains but does not reflect.

And then we pull underground again and everything goes black.

His parents both went crazy at the end of their lives. His father, my grandfather, would reel in fish from his hospital bed all day long. He would say, "Oh boy, this one's a real beauty," unhooking the invisible fish from its invisible hook.

Sometimes I sat next to his bed and pretended to hold a fishing pole. He would tell me where to cast my line, show me how to pull back on the pole and hold the reel until just the right moment before letting go. There in the hospital, holding our imaginary fishing poles, it almost seemed like we really were fishing together again, just like we used to do whenever I went to visit my grandparents in Idaho as a kid.

Grandpa Van Orman always made me feel like I was the best fisherwoman in the world. He used to sit next to me, catching and releasing his fish, saying, "too scrawny" or "too big" or "missing an eye," while I reeled in fish after fish. I kept going until he finally put his hand down firmly on my shoulder and said, "I think that's about enough, don't you think, kiddo? This will make a fine dinner for Grandma." I found out much later that all those years we had been fishing at the fish hatchery and he paid for the fish by the pound as we left.

We would take the fish back to the house and clean them off on a scaly workbench in the garage. They always slipped from my grasp in the basin of pink water, as though they were still alive and still trying to get away. My grandfather showed me how to grab the gills and cut down the center of the belly and then scoop along the inside of the fish with my hand, pulling out the innards. It was the part of fishing that I hated, but my grandfather always made me do it. He said, "Teach a man to fish, and he'll fish for a lifetime. Teach a man to gut and fry a fish, and only then will he eat for a lifetime."

Later, when I became a vegetarian and stopped fishing with my grandfather, I could sense his sadness and it gutted me.

He escaped the hospital once and they found him on the street, his hospital apron wide open in the back exposing his naked body, saying over and over, "What am I supposed to do? I've got nowhere to go. They've left me out here in the cold and I have no place to go." We never did figure out exactly who *they* were and how he got out. But I felt sad for him in that moment, felt sad for him being all alone inside that story. He really *was* alone with no place to go, I thought. Sometimes your own head can be the loneliest place on earth.

After he died, my grandmother said that he visited her at night. She said he slept next to her in the bed every night and it was just like it always was. And then one day he either wasn't there anymore, or she stopped talking about it. She stopped talking about it around the same time she sold the house in Jerome and moved to Salt Lake City to be closer to her kids.

A few years later, I helped take care of my grandmother while she was dying. I slept at her condo sometimes. She lived in an assisted living community by Aunt Kathy's house. The hospice nurse came and checked on her periodically, but the family liked to have someone there with her all the time, just in case.

In some ways, dementia seemed to free her mind. She told me about the time my father and his twin brother lit a barn on fire and then ran back home and pretended like nothing happened. She told me about washing and drying all their diapers by hand when they were babies and about being bit by a rabid coyote when she was a little girl.

But most of what she said was crazy. She would make up these elaborate math games, directing me to think of a number and then double it and multiply it and then she would tell me to take the number and put it in a lake or throw it out the window and the answer would become more and more elusive.

Once, not long before she moved permanently to the hospital, she called to me late at night. I was on the couch in the other room, reading. When I came into her room, she asked me to put my hands around her neck. "Just like this," she said, circling her own clumsy hands around her thin, veiny neck. I wondered what the hospice nurse would think if she walked into the room to see me with my hands around my grandmother's neck like that. I told her no, I wouldn't do it. But she asked again, this time almost crying. "Please," she said, "just for a minute. Just put your hands around my neck." I didn't know what to do. She seldom asked for anything. So I finally walked over to the side of the bed and put my hands lightly on her neck. It felt cold and geographic; I could feel through her skin to the veins and slack muscles, could feel the slow pumping of blood. It was scary to hold my grandmother like that. I only did it for a moment and then I released, not just my hands, but things inside, too. She said "thank you" and started to cry.

As we walk along the Charles back to my apartment, my father suddenly remembers being there twenty years before. He points to the building where he lived and says, "I used to look out my window every morning and watch the early morning rowers. They cut through the water in perfect sync. I remember one time they were rowing straight toward this flock of ducks. I was sure the boat was going to slice right through them. The rowers didn't slow down a bit. I could hardly bear to watch I was so scared for those poor little ducks. But then, at the very last minute, the very last *second*, the ducks parted right down the middle. Like it was no big deal."

When we get back to my apartment, we make sandwiches and then my dad falls asleep on the couch. I sit next to him, just as I did with his father and his mother. As we sit, he slips in and out of sleep, letting his neck drift back and then jerking it forward again, a motion they call *pescando* in Portuguese, or fishing.

His head finally tilts slowly back until it's resting on the back of the couch. His neck is long and exposed. It looks younger stretched back like that. I love how people look a different age when they sleep. It's a strong neck. It holds a lifetime.

Chairs

It started because Jimmy whined that Jonny was sitting in his chair.

"Well, it doesn't have your name written on it, does it?" our father said.

So then Jimmy went off and found a permanent marker and wrote his name incorrectly, "Jimy," on the underside of the chair. He turned the chair over to show our father and said, "It has my name on it. See?"

Our father looked like he was going to get angry, but then he just shook his head and said, "Okay, then."

Over the years we each added our own name to the bottom of a chair. Even our parents did it. The chairs traveled around the house with us. We took them into the living room to watch television, used them as stepladders to rummage through forbidden cupboards, positioned them strategically so we could hop from one to the other when we pretended that the floors were made of hot lava. At dinnertime we went searching for our chairs, sliding under the chairs on our backs, like car mechanics, to find the one that belonged to us.

We had eight chairs before we had eight people in the family. My parents got them at a garage sale. All of the chairs had brown vinyl seats and matching pieces of wood down the center of their backs that looked like the silhouette of a woman.

The chairs looked the same from a distance and then, as you got closer, you started to notice tiny differences—hairline scratches in the wood, L- and T-shaped tears in the vinyl. Like us with our slightly different noses and shades of blond hair. I have tiny threads of yellow in my irises.

Sometimes I imagined the formation of our family as a game of musical chairs, with me barely sliding into the last seat after the music stopped. I wondered what kid in heaven didn't make it into our family because I got his seat. I felt a simultaneous pride and guilt about that.

Now, home from my first year of college, I look for my chair. I spot it easily now because there is a cross-shaped crack on the vinyl seat and a little bit of cotton batting showing through.

I still turn the chair over to make sure it really is mine.

Once we were on the front page of the newspaper sitting in those chairs. We looked at the newspaper clipping a lot over the years because it fell out from between the pages of the photo album every time we opened it.

The picture was taken the Thanksgiving after Sara left for college so one of the chairs was empty somewhere, off camera. I was six years old. We sat with forks and knives clenched upright in our fists, checkered napkins tucked at our necks, a turkey in the center of the table, our chairs receding toward the vanishing point. The caption below the photo said that our father was "a Mormon Pastor." We all laughed hysterically about that later.

Who took the picture and why was it in the paper? No one remembers. Our memories of that year were filled with different newspaper articles. It was the Thanksgiving before Mrs. Rojas died.

I do have a memory of Thanksgiving the following year. The Rojas kids came over to eat with us. They came over a lot during the months of their father's trial, though not as much as before. They were still living with the Robinsons. When they came over we turned off the television and built forts outside, sledded down our stairs on a twin mattress, jumped off the roof onto the trampoline. On Thanksgiving we ate shish kabobs, which we had never done before.

We grilled them outside and then played a game of soccer. It was not a game of us against them. We merged them with our family first and then we divided into two teams. It didn't matter who won. We didn't take any pictures that day that I know of. I wish we had.

After their father went to prison we saw less and less of the Rojas kids. They moved to a different neighborhood with the Robinsons. My mother told me later that she and my father had offered to adopt them but Mrs. Rojas's family wanted them to go to a Catholic family. My mother said she understood. She said that if something happened to her and my dad she would want us to go to a Mormon family.

Around the time we moved to Utah, they moved to Miami to live with some distant relatives they had there. We wrote them letters. The letters didn't come back to us but we didn't get any responses from them either. Utah was the vanishing point.

My mother brought home two chairs from the estate sale after Mrs. Rojas died, along with a stained oak armoire. The chairs were embroidered with roses. Both of them broke within a month. They were too fragile to withstand our household. I felt a little relieved when the chairs were gone. They had never seemed like they were ours, I guess because she never had a chance to give them to us. We used the armoire for years. It didn't bother me the way the chairs did. It hadn't held her body. The armoire was heavy, ugly, and resilient. Once, several years after we moved across the country and the armoire went into the guest bedroom, I found a dark curly hair in one of the drawers. No one in our family had hair like that. I wondered if it could have been hers. It felt strange seeing a little piece of her after all those years.

When we got the Internet at our house for the first time I searched for them. I found an article in a Florida newspaper saying that Dr. Rojas, who was now Mr. Rojas, wanted to be Dr. Rojas again. He was out of prison. It didn't say what happened to the kids.

He made the news and she got buried deeper. My heart fluttered unevenly when I read his name, the same name as my first crush, almost like the skip of being in love, but not. I guess like the way crying shares a border with laughter. My heart has fluttered the same way my whole life since I was seven, every time I hear of a murder, anywhere. It fluttered like that right after she died and my brothers told me to wear a wig and sunglasses whenever I went outside because, "He might come back for us."

I am sitting now in the chair in the office. This chair is different from the eight kitchen chairs. It's cut from a different kind of wood, though I wouldn't know what kind. It's taller and its curves are in different places. It stays in the office, firmly planted in front of the desk. The only time it gets moved is when we vacuum the carpet beneath it. The chair always gets put back in exactly the same spot. We know it's the same spot because of the indentations its legs have made into the carpet. A million sweeps of the vacuum won't fluff it up again. It's brown or black, depending on the light. The chair is heavy but elegant somehow. Its seat is covered with deep scratches that have softened with time, almost like a wound that has healed, and scarred. It makes the chair seems like a living thing, capable of sickness and recovery.

The chair has sat each of us in turn as we've stayed up late working on homework assignments, waited for phone calls from boyfriends and girlfriends, secretly listened in on said phone calls from boyfriends and girlfriends, rummaged through desk drawers looking for clues about whether our parents really are who they say they are. I feel comfortable in this chair, more comfortable, perhaps, than in my own signed chair.

"When did we get this chair anyway?" I ask my mother, who is paused in the doorway looking at me, as she has periodically done since I got back from Hawaii. "It seems like we've had it forever."

"Oh, that chair belonged to Aurelia Rojas," my mother says. "She was having a yard sale one Saturday after the divorce. She was tight for money, I think. I asked her how much she wanted for the chair but she shook her head and told me she wanted me to have it. I tried to insist on paying for it, but she said all she wanted was for it to go to a good home. I know it's not in style, but I just haven't been able to get rid of it," she says. "It reminds me of her."

The chair has been here all this time. I sat on it for years without realizing that it had belonged to Mrs. Rojas. I wonder whether I would have sat on it differently if I had known. I feel the chair sticking to the backs of my thighs. It must have stuck to the backs of her thighs on the hottest days, too.

This one belongs to all of us.

Curfew

On my wedding night, my father wakes my mother up in the middle of the night and asks, "Is Lisa home yet?"

Expecting

We are driving in the Big Blue Van and I ask my mother, "How do you get a baby?"

She pauses and then says, "Well, when you're old enough and you're married, you pray for Heavenly Father to give you one."

"But then what?" I ask.

And she says, "That's all."

"But why did you and Dad get six babies?" I ask. "How did that happen?"

"Because that's how many Heavenly Father wanted us to have," she says.

We are going in circles.

I begin praying for babies. I pray that God will give me as many children as he would like me to have, but preferably four. I pray that I will get married when I am twenty-one so I can start having kids when I am twenty-two, like my mother. I pray that I will meet someone whose last name is "Heart" so we can be the Heart Family, like my new favorite Barbie dolls. I finally save up enough money and buy Mom Heart and Dad Heart but I don't have enough money for the twins yet. I will have four children, two boys and two girls. A set of boy and girl twins first, and then I will space the others two years apart to give them the highest chance of being friends. Not so close that they compete with one another, but not so far apart that they can't relate to each other. They will all have blond hair and blue eyes, like me, like Mom Heart and Dad Heart. They will be smart, funny, adventurous, and very attractive, but they will act as if they aren't any of those things. They will, after all, be modest and humble.

I want to be exactly like my mother.

I learn to do counted cross-stitch and I start with one that says, "Love at Home," with a picture of a little house with two windows and a red front door and a line of red hearts between the words and the house. My mother helps me attach lace around the edge of the cross-stitch frame and thread a light blue ribbon through the eyelets. I make cross-stitches from my mother's pattern books and give them to my friends for their birthdays. They have sayings on them like "Bless This Mess!" and "Count Your Blessings and Your Calories!" My friends look confused when they open their gifts. "Um, thanks" they say, smacking their gum and tossing the cross-stitch, still half wrapped, to the ground. Their mothers give them sympathetic looks that say, "We'll take care of it later." A few days later I see my counted cross-stitch hanging above the stove in their kitchen or in the guest bathroom. All my friends care about is pierced ears and having their own telephones in their rooms.

After dinner I watch Nick at Nite by myself on the little television in my parents' room until they come in and tell me it's time for bed. I watch *The Donna Reed Show, Mr. Ed, My Three Sons* and *The Dick Van Dyke Show* if they let me stay up late enough. I wonder why I couldn't have been born thirty years earlier.

My mother teaches me to knit baby hats and I imagine the little heads I will slip into them some day. I crochet baby booties and imagine tiny feet with ten toes and toenails that look like miniature half moons.

I play Barbies with my best friend, Emily. We take Mom Heart and Dad Heart's clothes off and lay them together on the bed because Emily says that's how babies are made. After they lay on the bed for a few minutes, they suddenly have a baby. Actually, they suddenly have a teenager named Skipper. I still haven't saved up enough money for the twins.

At church they tell us that no success can compensate for failure in the home. They tell us that someday we will be mothers and there is no higher calling than God trusting us with his children. I believe this.

When people ask what I'd like to be when I grow up, I say, "a mother" and sometimes I say, "a mother and a writer." I tell them I will write when my kids are taking naps and then, later, when they are in school. I reference Mary Higgins Clark, whose mysteries I take from my mother's bookshelf and begin reading when I am nine. I tell them how she wrote at five o'clock in the morning, before her children woke up. My mother takes me to see Mary Higgins Clark at a book signing at the mall when I am ten and I wait in line for hours to meet her. When we get close enough, I see that she is really old and that she wears a lot of makeup and fancy jewels. This is not the way I had pictured her. I give her my copy of *Loves Music, Loves to Dance* to sign and she writes, "Lisa, keep reading!" I am not impressed. My mother says that she was probably tired from signing all those books and not to take it personally. I take it personally.

I make lists of my favorite baby names. Every year I cross off the ones I no longer like and add new ones. I ask for a book of baby names for Christmas when I am eleven. I tell my parents it is to help me name the characters in my stories, but really it's for exactly what it's supposed to be for: baby names. I try out first names and middle names together, figuring out the right combination of sounds and syllables.

The summer between sixth and seventh grades, my new best friend Becca and I take a childcare class at the hospital. Our mothers drop us off every Wednesday for four weeks and we learn how to take care of newborns. We learn how to change their diapers, feed them, what to do when they cry ("Do *not* shake them! Do *not* drop them! Treat them like you would treat a delicate egg! You do *not* want to break the egg!"). We practice on dolls. I wonder what we are actually learning since there is no actual poop to wipe off the babies' bottoms and they don't cry. They aren't even like the dolls at the toy store that drink from a bottle and wet their pants. We practice CPR, tilting their heads back and using two fingers to pump their diaphragms while we breathe into their little plastic mouths. The air has nowhere to go, so it just goes right back into our mouths. We do the Heimlich on the baby dolls, positioning them facedown over our knees and carefully pressing on their backs. I get a certificate at the end of the course verifying that I can be trusted to take care of real, actual children.

My friends start a babysitters' club and they tell me that I can be the alternate alternate officer. This means that if there is a babysitting job and the president, vice president, secretary, treasurer, and alternate officer can't do it, I get the job. I have never gotten the job.

Finally my next-door neighbor offers to pay me a dollar an hour to watch her four kids. They have a crawling baby. I wonder what I am supposed to do with the baby when I need to go the bathroom. Should I leave her outside the door or bring her in? What if I do bring her into the bathroom with me and the parents come home at that very moment and think it's weird? Should I ask them questions like this? I decide that no, I should not.

When I tuck the kids into bed, I sing to them. I sing a song my father used to sing to annoy his older sister when she was practicing the piano, with the same surprise ending:

Good morning, merry sunshine,
How did you wake so soon?
You chased away the little stars,
And shone away the CRICKIES!

Then I take them on a magic carpet ride like my mother used to do. I tell them to close their eyes and then I tell them that a magic carpet has just pulled up in front of their house. Even though the carpet looks small, it somehow fits all of us comfortably with room to spare. I take them around the world on the carpet, to places I've read about. I take them to Fatu-Hiva and Easter Island because I have recently become infatuated with the adventure books of Thor Heyerdahl. I take them to a farm in Vermont and to Disney World. I don't take them to Panama City Beach, or to Mr. Surf's to eat red beans and rice with the Polish family who owns it, or to the little sandy spot beside the Show-N-Tail where Emily and I used to smoke candy cigarettes because those are places I want to save for my own kids.

After they fall asleep, I go into their rooms and put a hand on their chests to make sure they are still breathing because wouldn't it be just my luck that they would die of SIDS on my watch. I pray that God please won't let them die of SIDS while I'm babysitting.

I am relieved when the parents walk through the door at the end of the night and I can walk across the lawn to my own house where I am the child.

I get a babysitting job for another neighbor. They tell me they have something new called the Internet and that I can use it after the baby goes to sleep. I do not know what to do on the Internet. My friend told me you can ask it anything you want, so I type in "when will I get my period?" and "how do I get a boy to kiss me?" and then decide the Internet is boring and turn on the television. I can't wait for the parents to get back so I can go home. The parents drive me home and ask me if I would like to sit for them again. I say, "no?" It comes out weird like that, a question. I don't know why I say it. It's not what I meant to say, but I'm too embarrassed to retract it. They never call me to sit for them again and I'm surprised and disappointed.

In ninth grade I take a childhood development class. We are given a ten-pound bag of sugar that we are supposed to pretend is a baby. We have to draw a face on it and put a diaper on it and take it with us everywhere we go. After a few days, the edges of the bag get worn out from keeping the sugar baby in my backpack and sugar starts seeping out of one corner—slowly at first and then faster. The sugar comes out of the diaper and makes a trail wherever I go. Every day I lose more and more sugar. By the end of the week, all I have is an empty sack with a few granules of sugar rattling around in the bottom. I fail the class. "But it was a bag of sugar!" I say to the teacher. She shakes her head and gives me a look that makes me feel like I have failed as a mother.

Every day after school I get a big bowl of baby carrots and secretly watch Oprah on the basement TV.

Every little thing my mother does starts to annoy me. I hate the way she licks her lips when she is writing a check. I hate the way she says "guysies," the way she says her ancestors are "Welch," the way she pronounces the word "huge" without the h.

I decide I want to be nothing like my mother.

I never did save up enough money to buy the twins. They don't even make those dolls anymore.

Sara has a baby when I am seventeen and she lets me into the room to watch. I get queasy and have to sit on the recliner with my head between my legs.

By the time I reach twenty-two I begin to worry that I will never get married. My mother was married and pregnant with Sara by now. My mother begins to get worried, too. She asks me if I want her to teach me how to hold a boy's hand. She tells me that once she dated a guy without hormones and asks me whether I have hormones. I say, "Mom, you know how peanut butter and chocolate are the perfect combination? I am peanut butter looking for my chocolate. I just haven't found my chocolate yet."

I am bad at love. I get engaged and unengaged (disengaged?), twice. I am not usually this fickle. I know what I want, but I don't know how to get it.

My mother changes her tune. She says, "Don't get married unless you are really, really in love. Marriage is hard enough when you love each other."

I meet Dan when I am least expecting it. I walk past him at a wedding and he says, "Hey, don't I know you from somewhere?" He doesn't look familiar but I say, "I don't know, maybe?" because I am there alone and have no one else to talk to except for the bride and groom, who are busy. I sit down next to him and we talk all night. When the bride throws the bouquet, I catch it without even trying. It practically hits me in the face. All the men scatter when the garter is tossed; they want nothing to do with it. Dan, being a good sport, goes and picks it up off the floor.

At the end of the night, he says, "Hey, what if I never see you again?"

I say, "Oh, I'm sure we'll see each other around." It's not what I want to say, but I don't want to seem overzealous.

He says, "Well, can I get your number to make sure I see you again?"

I write my number on the back of an appointment card for my optometrist. I realize after leaving the wedding that I don't have the appointment written anywhere else. I'm eager for his phone call, not only because I like him, but also so he can tell me the day and time of my next vision exam.

He does call, nearly a week later. He tells me he wanted to call sooner but he didn't want to seem overzealous.

When he comes to pick me up for our first date, at my parents' house where I still live, my mother gasps audibly when she answers the door. She leans into the living room, where I am sitting and mouths, "CHOCOLATE."

I have no idea what she is talking about until I walk to the door and see that he is wearing a sweatshirt that says "Chocolate" on it. He tells me later that it is the name of his favorite skateboard company. We drive to a sushi restaurant in his mother's station wagon. He still lives at home, too. After we eat, we drive up into the mountains and I show him a cave I found a few weeks ago while I was hiking. In the dark of the cave, I know this is it. I can feel him feeling it, too. He reaches out and grabs my hand.

I did not expect falling in love to be so cliché: the pick up lines, the phone number slid into the wallet, meeting at a *wedding*, the sweatshirt. Gosh, God must think I am such an idiot; he literally has to spell everything out for me. And then there is the giddiness I feel, like some dumb movie. I am stunned by love, suddenly and completely, like a gunshot in the back. I am almost embarrassed by the simplicity of it—the one thing I was expecting to be so hard ends up being the easiest thing in the world. I guess that's why it is called falling in love, an absence of control. Although this feels more like rising. Like cold bread dough suddenly placed in a warm room.

We get married on a rainy day in December. I take this as a good omen because I have always loved the rain. I am twenty-five. On the other side of the wedding, it feels like such a young age to be married. I imagine my mother, who already had three kids by now. I'm not ready to have a baby yet. I want to learn how to live with a man and do my own taxes for the first time in my life. I want to live in a new city together and to know what that sounds like against the sounds of all the other places I've lived.

We move to Boston.

When we do start trying a couple of years later, it feels a little reckless and out of control, like the first time my father let go of the back seat of my bicycle and I realized I was pedaling alone. I'm ready, or pretending to be ready, but I'm not ready. It is a thing I didn't realize fully until my feet were on the pedals, circling round and round. Everyone is looking at me so expectantly. Don't fall.

I am sure it will happen immediately. I have followed my mother's formula to a T: I got old enough, I got married, I prayed for the baby. I even did extra things she did not mention on our car ride all those years ago. The things they taught me in health class about how babies are made.

Finally, after months and months of checkmarks and wrong answers, Dan and I see a doctor. The doctor puts an ultrasound wand on my stomach and then shoots blue dye into me. I always expected to have an ultrasound in another setting, a situation in which my stomach is round and verdurous. When the dye doesn't pour out of my fallopian tubes, as it should, the doctor says in his thick accent, "Your fallopian tubes are obstructed."

"What?" I say.

He says it again. "Your fallopian tubes are blocked off. You have what is called a hydrosalpinx." *Hydro Salpinx*. Water trumpet. It's all Greek to me. I understand the words, but I don't understand the words. Trumpets cannot be played underwater. Can they? I need air. I feel like my ninth grade bag of sugar, emptying slowly until all that is left is the crinkled waxed bag inside a bag with a few useless granules rattling around in the bottom of it.

I feel tricked by my body. It always acted like it had all its parts in working order. It looked like a body on the outside.

I feel like I felt when I saw my grandmother's wig on the dresser.

"You have to have surgery to remove them," the doctor says. "And then in vitro. You have to do in vitro."

I am stuck on the word *in vitro*. In glass. I suddenly feel like I am a child again looking at the baby Barbie dolls behind the glass case at the toy store. I put my face up against the glass, staring at the little button noses and plastic faces. My mother always, eventually, grabbed my hand and told me gently that it was time to go. Why couldn't I ever save up enough money to buy those damn dolls? I am Skipper, trapped in a perpetual adolescence.

I change back into my clothes, trembling.

When I come out of the room, Dan tells me that while I was changing the doctor found him in the hallway and said, "Your wife is in there getting dressed. She was very good." He tells me, with a laugh, that he wonders what, exactly, went on in there. I laugh, too. But all I can think about is all those years I spent expecting the wrong thing.

Later, I take the car out and drive in circles around my block. I call my mother on the phone. "I have news," I say. "I went to the doctor today and he said I'm not going to have a baby."

"What?" she says and then I hang up.

At night, I dream of test tube babies, their round faces pressed up against the glass, looking at me. I want to let them out, but the glass case is locked and I don't have the key. They look so fragile and expectant in there.

This is the tragedy of glass: you can see what you want, but you can't have it.

Glass Flowers

I am wandering around a museum, pretending to read the little placards but not really reading them, focusing my eyes on nothing, as I often find myself doing in museums. It is an immaturity left over from my childhood. My brain screams "boring!" before I've even set foot in the exhibition halls.

But then I find myself suddenly in a room full of flowers, and my eyes begin to focus. The flowers are made of glass, but they don't look like glass. The plaque on the wall says that the collection was created by a father and a son near Dresden. I begin to imagine them working together on a workbench like my father's, cold painting stems and petals, occasionally stopping to admire one another's work. The flowers look so real in their perpetual bloom. I sidestep from flower to flower, like a bee on a pollinating spree. As I read the description cards and look at the anatomy of the flowers, I am surprised by how similar their reproductive organs are to my own: ovaries, tubes, stigma.

And then I see this one flower. The flower looks normal, as healthy as a glass flower can look, but the card says that its organs are incomplete. It's missing an ovary. Suddenly, I don't care about any of the other flowers. I care only about this one. I stop and look at the flower for a long time, thinking about what Georgia O'Keefe said about taking a flower in your hand and making it your world. Except I am in a museum and they won't let me take it in my hand.

I know the flower is glass, but it seems impossible that there is no life in it. I see it taking in sunlight and maturing, expecting something beautiful to happen to it. It is still waiting.

Artifact

I am the i,
caught between
art and fact.

Mother

My mother and I have the opposite problem. She kept having babies each year until she figured out that you can, in fact, get pregnant while breastfeeding.

But I have a dead sea in me. My fallopian tubes are closed off and bursting from their casings like a pair of sausages.

She had no time for herself.

And I have all the lonely time in the world.

Making Sandwiches with My Father

1.

The summer before my sophomore year of high school, he teaches me how to make a Reuben. We assemble ingredients, get them ready so we can add each one as quickly as possible because we must eat the sandwich while it is still hot and the top of the bread is crispy. I learn his tricks: drain the sauerkraut well ("nothing worse than a soggy sandwich"), use just the right amount of butter on the outsides of the bread, choose the very best Thousand Island dressing you can find because it makes or breaks the sandwich.

When we talk, it is only about the sandwiches.

Reubens have become our art form; he cooks while I drain and assemble. For a while in the summer we eat a Reuben together every day at noon.

My mother is alarmed by this. She plugs her nose at the smell of the sauerkraut, her face wrinkles in disgust at the corned beef. Her taste is not distinguished enough for such things.

By my senior year we are making our own bread and pickling our own cabbage. We corn our own beef. We find recipes for Thousand Island dressing in gourmet recipe books and we add our own secret ingredients, making it even better.

2.

When I am twenty-three, I break up with my fiancé while my parents are in Alaska. I am alone in their house and I spend three days crying, watching comedies and taking droplets of St. John's Wort. I leave the house once to buy groceries for this man I was going to marry because he lost his job the week before I broke up with him. The two events are unrelated, but still I feel bad.

On the third day, my parents get home, all smiles. They have brought home a cooler full of salmon and an ulu knife. My eyes are still puffy and I can taste the bitterness of St. John's Wort on my tongue as I sit them down on the couch and tell them that there will be no wedding. They say nothing. Nothing. You could slice the silence with the ulu my mother has just given me. And then, finally, my father stands up and says, "Well, I'm hungry. I'm going to go make myself a Reuben."

3.

I am twenty-five years old and on the couch in the basement when the phone rings. My father always picks up on the first ring. I hear his heavy footsteps above me as he walks over and picks up the phone in the kitchen and says "Hello." Everything reverberates down here in the basement, where I have been spending a lot of my time lately. My feet and hands are cold. They are always cold. I inherited that from my mother.

He says the following things:

"What time?"

"Was anyone there?"

"Do you want me to call anyone?"

"Okay, thanks for calling."

"Bye."

He says these things in the same tone of voice that he would say, "The printer is out of paper."

He hangs up and walks to the top of the stairs. "Lisa!" he yells and I say "What?" and he says, "Grandma died."

My feet and hands are very cold. I have already forgotten how she smells. And now I am thinking about how she always told me to chew with my mouth closed. I want to blister with tears, want to sob into my freezing cold hands for her. But I don't. I guess my father and I are the same that way. I wonder, as I always wonder in times like these, if I loved my grandma enough. And that answer, more than anything, scares me.

I go upstairs and my father is in the kitchen making a Reuben. So I go in and I make a Reuben, too, and we eat.

4.

We're on the train. My parents are in Boston for the weekend. My father is looking out the window and my mother and I are talking about his mind. How it's going.

My mother has just told me that she took him in for an MRI and some tests. The doctor asked him what day of the week and what month it was and he couldn't remember.

And then, in the middle of our conversation, I look down at my hands and I notice that there is dirt beneath my fingernails. And I know it's crazy, but the dirt makes me cry. I remember how my father used to clean under my fingernails with his Swiss army knife during church. He took my little fingers in his hands and slid the blade under each nail. I loved to watch the black wipe away like that and then come off on the knife. He got so close to the skin and it hurt a little, but I didn't mind.

When we get home, we are hungry, so I decide to make us Reubens. My father butters the outside of the rye bread while the pan is heating up and I drain the sauerkraut. We don't talk. He layers the sandwiches skillfully: corned beef, Swiss, sauerkraut, Thousand Island. My father—he doesn't miss a beat.

When we sit down at the table, I watch my father as he bites into his sandwich.

"Oh, that's good!" he says. "What is that?"

I say, "That's your favorite sandwich, Dad."

And he says, "Yes, I suppose it is."

A Real Character

My mother called me the other day. The first thing she said was, "Don't be mad when I ask this."

And of course I immediately got mad.

"Don't be mad," she said again, "but do you have any stories where I don't look like a complete idiot?"

"But the mother is my favorite character!" I say.

And that's the honest truth.

The Ellens

My father has been talking lately about all the Ellens.

"Boy there sure are a lot of Ellens!" he says.

He tells me that his driver's name is Ellen. She does all the driving because she needs him to navigate. He sits up front with her. She is not very good with directions, especially for a driver. He would rather be behind the wheel, but she needs his help from the passenger seat so he obliges.

His cook, also an Ellen, comes in to make him breakfast, lunch and dinner. She knows that he likes an ice cube at the bottom of his bowl, then granola, then raisin bran, then skim milk. She knows that he likes to eat it with a big spoon. She doesn't cook a lot of meat. He wishes she would though. He likes to eat roast beef with horseradish.

There is a woman named Ellen he doesn't like much. He thinks she may be in law enforcement. She won't let him do a lot of things. He suspects that she might also be stealing from him. Things have gone missing. Pocket knives, mechanical pencils, masking tape. He keeps these things in the pockets of his jeans now. He has started to sleep in the jeans, too, because night is ripe for stealing.

An Ellen comes in at night. She sits up with him as he waits for his ride to come. The other Ellen, the driver, always seems to be running late.

He almost doesn't mind though because he has become good friends with this night Ellen. She helps him take the things out of his pockets and count them to make sure it is all there. Sometimes when he is with this Ellen he decides not to go out at all. They have such a good time together. He puts his head on her shoulder and hopes that his wife won't mind.

His wife's name is Ellen.

When he tells her about all the Ellens, she says, "Well, which one do you like best?"

He looks at her, laughs a little, and says, "Well, I guess you."

Cities of Sugar and Salt

My mother tells me that she spent hours the other day driving my father around, looking for a grocery store by the train tracks. He was very insistent. "My life has gotten very bizarre," my mother laughs.

Later, when his twin brother called (he calls every Sunday morning now, at eleven), he told my mother that the grocery store by the tracks is in Sugar City, Idaho, where they lived when they were toddlers.

In the time they circled around Salt Lake looking for the grocery store, they could have driven to Sugar City, three and a half hours away. I wonder whether the grocery store is still there, whether the train is still running.

It is a small glitch, really. This issue of time. My father's memory makes the past present. He is where he was.

Sugar and salt *do* look the same, after all.

How to Draw a Body: Sketches with My Mother

"I want you to draw me a picture of what's wrong with you," my mother says.

She says this to me in the bathroom, the one she shares with my father, after I find her crying over a tampon I have not buried deep enough in the shreds of tissue and cardboard rolls in the wastebasket, the can's can as we used to call it.

"What?" I say.

"Don't be mad with me," she says.

"Okay," I say, "I need to go." I begin to unzip my pants so she'll get the hint. She steps out of the door frame and into her bedroom and I close and lock the door behind her.

She slides a steno pad and a red mechanical pencil under the bathroom door.

I want her to go away. I will stay in here, drinking from the faucet and making toilet paper origami, for as long as it takes.

Here's the real problem: I don't know where to begin. In this, in everything in my whole life, I don't know how to make something from nothing. Someone else needs to get things started. Someone needs to make that first squiggle on the paper.

Here's the other problem: the problem of what's wrong with me. Really, it's the same problem. Where to begin?

I'll tell you a story: Once my girlfriends and I missed a flight from Hawaii back to the mainland because I didn't know how to read military time. My father worked for the military. I should have known better.

We couldn't get a flight out until the next morning. We were broke and stranded so someone's mother arranged for us to stay with a woman she used to know who lived somewhere just outside of Honolulu. The taxi dropped us off on a street lined with "Keep Out" and "Beware of Dog" signs. The address we were given had a cardboard sign attached to the chain-link fence. Someone had scribbled the words "trespassers will be persecuted" on it.

When we knocked on the door, a middle-aged woman came out. She spoke in a terrifying voice that I will never forget. The voice was low and choppy, robotic. Before we could get through the front door, she shoved an informational pamphlet out to us and said, "Here's what's wrong with me."

Sometimes I wish I had a pamphlet to hand out to everyone I come in contact with; a pamphlet with bullet points explaining all the things that are wrong with me so we can just get it out of the way.

When we were kids we were sent to the bathroom as punishment. My parents sent us there instead of our bedrooms so we couldn't complain about having to go to the bathroom or needing a drink of water. We were sent to the downstairs bathroom, the one without a tub, the blandest bathroom in the house. I remember the time I found a box of tampons under the sink and how it felt like Christmas, a box full of little pink and white presents waiting to be opened. I unwrapped them one by one and then shot each tampon out of its cardboard applicator like a rocket. When my time was up and my mother finally opened the door to let me out, she found me in a heap of paper wrappers and disassembled parts on the floor, grinning. I asked her what those things were and she said, "I'll tell you when you're older."

She never did.

This is one thing I want to tell my mother: that my head feels plugged with tampon, stuffed with cotton, empty and full at the same time.

Now, in the master bathroom, I do what I always did back then: I open drawers, cabinets, look at all the medications, look for secrets. My parents' bathroom cabinets are stuffed with medications. The funny thing is, we don't really take any of them. We pride ourselves on our excellent health and our ability to withstand pain. I remember being sick for days as a kid before my mother offered me some aspirin. She pulled the bottle out of a cabinet and said, "Well, you could try this and see if it does anything." When I took it, I felt amazing.

Last year, the last time I was home, I threw away a bottle of expired ibuprofen. It was from a drugstore that wasn't in business anymore, a drugstore that had been closed for more than a decade. There were other, more recent bottles of ibuprofen, enough ibuprofen to last a lifetime.

My father was furious when he found the bottle in the wastebasket. He yelled, "I will decide what will get thrown away!" and then he took the bottle out of the wastebasket and put it back on the shelf.

I open the drawers in the vanity and try on my mother's liquid foundation and her lipstick. The lipstick is a cheap pharmacy brand, a lackluster mauve. I have just started to wear lipstick, at thirty, for the first time in my life. I bought it on my way home from the doctor's office, after he showed my husband and me the ultrasound pictures of my fallopian tubes and explained what's wrong with me. My husband took the train home and I drove to the mall and tried on expensive lipsticks at the department store counter. I kept applying and wiping off lipsticks until I found the perfect shade of red with blue undertones, *Shanghai Express*, the color of blood.

My mother and I have blue undertones. We need to wear lipstick with blue undertones because we are Summers. I look at myself in the mirror and remember my mother holding the *Color Me Beautiful* swatches with pinked edges up to my face when I was ten or eleven and saying, "Well, you might be a Spring, but I think you're probably a Summer, like me. Let's see how you look in peach." We look horrible in peach. It washes us out.

My mother and I are both Summers, pear-shaped, blue personalities, INFJs. When I was younger all our houseguests had to take the Myers-Briggs personality assessment after dinner. My mother would sit them down with the assessment while she cleared the table and put Cool Whip on the dessert. When they were finished with the test, she would have my father add up their answers. Then she would announce their outcomes and read them the chapter that described them while we ate dessert.

I remember when I took the test. I must have been eight or nine. My father had to explain some of the questions to me in terms that I could understand. I remember one question: "Would you rather be stuck in a rut or have your head in the clouds?" I didn't know what a rut was and my father explained that it was like feeling trapped, feeling like you couldn't pull yourself out of something. I couldn't imagine why anyone would choose that answer. To have your head in the clouds, I thought, was wonderful. I remember my mother reading my results and how thrilled she was that we were both INFJs: *I*ntroverted, I*n*tuitive, *F*eeling, *J*udging. We were, it said, a mere one percent of the world's population. My mother and I were creative geniuses, it said, puzzling, quiet, independent, intricately woven.

I remember wanting to be like my mother and not wanting it at the same time. Wanting to be all of those things, but alone.

My mother is still outside the door, asking if everything is okay in there. She asks if the toilet is clogged or if I'm not feeling well.

"I'm fine," I say.

Actually, I'm bored. I lift the lid from the tank on the back of the toilet. I know its anatomy inside and out. As an adult, I can fix almost anything that goes wrong with the toilet from all the hours I spent plumbing its depths as a kid. I lift the chain connected to the black rubber ball and watch all the water drain out. Then I put it down and watch the water rise back up to the proper level, marked by an orange-brown sludge line.

At some point I fall asleep wedged between the sink and the toilet. When I wake up, I wonder why I am always so tired. What's wrong with me? I fall asleep everywhere—on buses, in movie theatres, at parties. I even fell asleep in the dentist's chair one time, reclined and bibbed as if

I were about to crack open a lobster with all the little tools laid out neatly on the tray in front of me. I was only going to close my eyes for a minute because the light was so bright and because the dentist kept asking me questions that I couldn't answer with my mouth full of spit and pick and refuse. But once my eyes were closed it seemed impossible to open them again. It seemed like the hardest thing in the world.

I have always been this way. I used to beg my mother to put me to bed. "I'm so tired, Mommy. Can I *please* go to bed now?"

My mother, on the other hand, is an insomniac. Every night she tucks my father into bed, waits for him to fall asleep, and then climbs out of the bed and watches television until there is nothing left to watch but static and infomercials.

Maybe I will sketch a picture of myself sleeping in the bathroom for my mother. But I know that's not what she wants. She wants a picture of the inside. She wants me to draw my body, circle the problem areas, say: "This is what's wrong with me. This is why there is no baby."

It occurs to me that my mother doesn't know what the inside of a woman's body looks like. She has had babies, six of them, but she doesn't know. And why should she? She had sex, threw up a few times, watched her belly grow and then, nine months later, a baby came out.

I never paid attention in health class, either. *The Miracle of Life* video made me queasy. I had to put my head between my legs. You don't pay attention, not really, until the doctor sits you down and shows you the charts and says, "This is what's wrong with you."

I have run out of possibilities here in the bathroom, stuck in a rut. I have turned the faucet on and off, flushed the toilet and watched the cyclone of water swirl and then disappear down the hole into the body of the toilet. I've written the words *wash me* in mauve lipstick on the mirror.

I wonder if my mother is still out there. I put my ear up to the door and I think I can hear her sitting on the edge of the bed, breathing and maybe sighing.

I stare at the blank piece of paper and remember how we used to play Pictionary as a family on Sunday nights. My mother would pop a big bowl of popcorn and we would circle around the game board on the living room floor with our pencils and pads of paper.

Even though Jonny and Mark, the artists, almost always won, I loved being on a team with my mother. She was the worst artist in the family. She drew stick figures and licked her lips obsessively in concentration. I think I loved it because she would get so fired up. When you couldn't guess what she was drawing, she would take her little eraser-less stub of a pencil and point at what she'd drawn over and over again. Then she would start making all these muffled noises and jerky motions, like someone who has been tied up and gagged. We let her do it, even though it was against the rules, because it never helped anyway. It was just funny.

I put the pad of paper on the toilet seat and begin to sketch vigorously. It feels like Pictionary again—only the rules have changed slightly, with my mother on the other side of the door. I sketch a body, a woman's body. I draw breasts, ovaries, fallopian tubes, a vagina, the whole shebang. I draw the kind of picture that would have sent me to the bathroom when I was kid, but I'm already here, so what the hell. I slip the drawing under the door and start to explain:

"An egg is released from the ovaries every month. Usually, one month it is released from one side and the next from the other side."

I pause to make sure she's listening and then I say, "There are two ovaries."

"Okay, okay," she says, "but what does it look like inside of you?"

Drawing never really was my thing anyway.

I slide up right next to the door and I don't quite know why, but I start to tell my mother the first story that pops into my head. "Mom," I say, "remember when we came to you, complaining that there was nothing good on TV? Remember when we told you that every channel had some dumb space thing on it? And you ran to the TV, so excited? It was the landing of the first space shuttle. You told us that maybe we would go to outer space on our honeymoons some day or decide to live out there somewhere." I pause. "Everything seemed possible back then, Mom."

Here is the other half of that story: The first time I was ever left alone—an unusually cold Tuesday in January, two days after my seventh birthday.

One of the few times my mother let me stay home sick. It was the day the Challenger was launched and I was glued to the TV set. My mother ran to the store for something, maybe a bottle of Sprite to help settle my stomach. I guess she figured if she didn't tell me, I wouldn't even notice she had gone. And I probably wouldn't have. But then the Challenger blew up and I ran around the house calling for her, but she wasn't there.

Maybe life is like that, too. Maybe we only pay attention, really pay attention, when things are going very badly.

I flush the toilet one last time and come out of the bathroom.

A few months later, my mother comes to Boston to take care of me because I have to have my fallopian tubes taken out the same day my husband starts his first real job. My father comes, too, but he seems confused as to why they're here. He asks my mother every day when they're going home and every day my mother tells him again.

As I lay on the tissue-papered table, I feel light for the first time in months. My only job is to lay here and breathe in and out. Nothing else is expected of me.

When I wake up from surgery, I am so thirsty. I keep asking my mother for water, more water, and my mother brings it to me. I drink cup after cup. When I finally throw up all over myself in the bed, the nurse yells at my mother for giving me so much water. "But she kept wanting it," my mother says.

When they finally discharge me, I am doped up and I sleep almost all the time. I don't eat anything for days. My mother sits with me on the couch as I sleep. When I'm not sleeping, I'm in pain. My father has forgotten the surgery, but he can see I'm hurting, so he keeps coming over and asking me what's wrong.

I tell him I don't feel well and then he pats my head and says, "Well, I sure hope you feel better soon, sweetie."

One day he asks me if I want him to make me a toast house. When we were kids, he always made us toast houses when we were sick. He would butter the toast and then sprinkle cinnamon and sugar on it. Then he would cut it into strips and stack the pieces like a log cabin. I want him to make me a toast house so badly, but I can't keep anything down, so I tell him that's okay, thanks anyway.

In between sleeping, I stumble to the bathroom to vomit. I can barely walk; sometimes I have to crawl on my hands and knees. My mother follows me. She kneels down on the checkerboard floor next to me, next to the wastebasket full of empty prescription bottles. She brushes my hair away from my face and rubs my back as I heave into the toilet bowl.

And for these few seconds, kneeling on the floor with my mother, I feel whole again. All I can feel is my mother's hand on my back and the smooth curvature of porcelain in my hands. Tears roll down my face as I throw up, just like they did when I was a child. I think it has something to do with the way the tear ducts synchronize with the gag reflex to emit at the same time. A simultaneous flushing. I haven't been able to cry for years; my sadness is dry as a desert. Funny that now, when I finally do cry, it is purely physical.

It feels good just the same.

My mother labors with me. Hand on back, hand on toilet, we rise and fall together. I draw a breath, draw strength from the breath. My mother draws my body up off the bathroom floor.

A Story for My Mother

Once upon a time, there was a perfect mother. She was beautiful, smart, and kept an immaculate house. She always said the perfect thing at the perfect time. She never made any mistakes.

The only problem with her was that she was incredibly boring and everyone hated her.

The end.

Lost Things

We've lost teeth, for one thing. One hundred and sixty baby teeth among us, not counting wisdom teeth. Some of them fell out easily. When they didn't, my father gave us two options: the pliers or the door. Each choice inflicted its own particular kind of pain. The pliers bore a pain of certainty—the pain of knowing that once they were clamped down tight, the tooth would come out carefully, slowly, achingly. The door held a pain of surprise. My father would tie one end of a piece of string to the tooth and then tie the other end to a door handle. Then he would pretend to slam the door several times until he finally did it for real and the tooth would go with it. If we were lucky, the suddenness of it all would override any actual pain. I, thankfully, lost my first tooth at six while eating an apple in my parents' bedroom.

We've lost twenty-eight wisdom teeth collectively. Mine never grew in and I felt that I lost out on the experience of missing school, watching movies and eating popsicles all day long. My father suggested that I am a more evolved species, outgrowing the need for wisdom teeth altogether, which is strange because my father says he doesn't believe in evolution. His wisdom teeth were yanked out by the military when he was in his mid-twenties. He was given no anesthesia.

My father lost part of his right index finger on the band saw in the garage while making us a Barbie house one Christmas and then paraded the finger in front of my mother, who fainted.

Sara, after winning the Junior Miss pageant, lost the Miss Florida pageant.

We lost at least five cats and three dogs.

We've lost loved ones to cancer, drugs, dementia, accidents. We once lost a woman we loved to murder.

When we were kids, my mother lost her purse at least once a day. We were often late for things because of it. She would say frantically, "Kids, quick! I'll give a quarter to whoever finds my purse!" and then we would run off, pushing each other out of the way, so we could get to the purse first. We would finally find it tucked away in some messy corner of the kitchen or caged beneath an inverted laundry basket. At some point, we got smart and started hiding the purse so we could get a quarter. My mother, to my knowledge, never found out.

We've lost, over the years, the desire to hurt one another, compete for attention, be right all the time.

We've lost weight. Jimmy lost it before every wrestling match. Amy and Sara lost it in high school by sucking on ice cubes when they were hungry. My mother lost it by counting calories and eating carrots. My mother, Sara, and Amy lost it quickly after their babies came, fitting into their old jeans the week after they got home from the hospital. Since reaching adulthood, I've gained as much weight as I've lost.

We've lost four pregnancies.

I've lost countless embryos. Lost them to medical waste bins labeled "biohazard" because they didn't have enough cells or because they weren't symmetrical enough or because they were too fragmented. They've been frozen and thawed and I imagine that, like me, they just didn't like the cold. Dozens of others have been lost inside me, unable to attach to my uterine walls. I imagine them floating around in there, bumping into fallopian tubes that do not work, searching for what to do in this unnatural situation. How shocking it must be for them to go from Petri dish to body like pet store fish being plopped into a fishbowl of new water. In my mind, my uterus is an ocean, large and impenetrable, a Bermuda triangle for embryos. Once they are placed there by the physician, carefully squirted into just the right spot, they disappear forever, absorbed instead of nourished.

I've lost sleep thinking about where those embryos go. I wake up suddenly, in the middle of the night, and need to know whether they were absorbed into my uterine lining or whether they were expelled by my body. I need to know whether they came out in the toilet or landed on my underwear at night. I need to know the exact moment this happened. These are the things the nurse doesn't say. She doesn't talk about what really matters, like when was the exact moment of loss and what happens to all these things once we've lost them?

Sometimes we've had an overwhelming sense that we've lost something but, when pressed, can't describe exactly what it was. We've come to the slow realization that it's possible to lose things we've never had.

We've lost friends because we moved or they moved or because we said something mean or because their parents didn't want them playing with us because we were Mormons. I lost my best friend Emily when we moved to Utah.

In high school, Jonny lost control of the car and totaled it.

When he was five, we lost Mark at a truck stop in Tennessee. We were all the way to Arkansas by the time we realized that one of us was missing. While we were gone, the man behind the counter gave him a candy bar and a Coke and let him help pump gas. Mark remembers that as one of the best days of his life.

Sometimes growing up in a big family, it was easy to feel lost in the shuffle. Other times, though, we found comfort in being absorbed by the collective body. For example, when my father wanted to know: "Heavens to Betsy, which one of you got into the asbestos insulation in the attic?" No one said a word or ratted anyone out. The truth was, we all played in it together. The truth was, we didn't know what that fluffy stuff was when we jumped and rolled around in it.

We all, sooner or later lost our vision. Then we lost our glasses and our contact lenses.

Some of us lost our virginity on our wedding day. I'm not sure what the exact number is.

My father lost faith briefly in college. And maybe it's related, but all three boys lost faith at one time or another. The girls, though, we are unwavering.

We've lost ourselves in our work, our love lives, school. We've lost focus. We've lost homework assignments. Some of us have lost our patience and our tempers pretty easily. We get that from our father.

My father has lost brain mass. His cerebral cortex is shrinking—he's lost tissue, nerve cells, synapses. In other words, he's losing his marbles. He lost his sense of independence when they took away his driver's license. He admits, in moments of clarity, to feeling lost, confused, depressed. But then, a few minutes later, he forgets and all those bad feelings disappear again. I wonder whether there is a space, a locked room, somewhere in his brain where all those memories are kept or whether they are just gone. He has forgotten what year he was born, how many children he has, the names of his brothers and sisters. When I call him on the phone, I say, "Hello, Dad. It's Lisa. Your youngest daughter." He doesn't recognize my voice anymore.

We've had to grieve the loss of our father before we've lost him.

But my father has a tenderness to him now that he never had before. He comes up behind my mother and surprises her with kisses on the back of her neck. He says, "You are the most beautiful woman I have ever seen. Are we married?" He follows her around the house, wants to be near her all the time. He has lost the need to get ahead.

Sometimes we think we've lost things, only to find them again, or to realize that they were never missing in the first place. We've probably lost things and never even noticed they were gone. We have wondered: Do we only lose things if we realize they are missing? The meanings of all these things are sometimes lost on us.

We lost our cherry tree in the backyard several years ago. We thought it looked fine—it was still flowering and bearing fruit—but my father chopped it down and showed us the rot on the inside of the trunk. He said we were going to lose it sooner or later anyway, may as well cut our losses and make room to plant something else.

Names

I gave birth to twins, a girl and a boy. They were conceived immaculately in sterile glass. I have a picture of them as embryos before they were put back into my body, before I knew whether they would wilt or multiply. The embryos look like little flowers with their clear cells clustered together like petals.

In the hospital their bassinets were labeled simply "Baby A" and "Baby B."

We gave them the names Maud and Lars.

Maud is the oldest. She traveled down the birth canal and out the other end. Lars was delivered three-and-a-half hours later via emergency caesarian section.

Their last name is Hadley, which means "heather field."

Maud means "powerful battler." It is also a type of gray plaid coat worn by shepherds in Scotland. Her middle name is Emilia, which means "industrious." Her nicknames are Baby A, Maudie, Maudest, Maudlin. Lars calls her Ma.

Lars means "crowned with laurel." His middle name is Van Orman, which is also my middle name, and the middle name of both of my sisters. We shifted the name up a slot when we got married, sandwiched it between our given names and our new foreign-sounding married names.

Our father used to tell us that Van Orman means "from the sea." I'm pretty sure he made that up. It used to make me mad, but now I don't care. A name means whatever you want it to mean. I read once that half of the Netherlands, where the name comes from, is below sea level and the other half is above it. Someday I will tell Lars that Van Orman means "from the sea and the mountains." Liberties have always been taken with the name, anyway.

Lars's nicknames are Baby B, Lasse, Lars Poetica, Van. Maud calls him Sha.

Their first word was Papa, which is what they call my father. He does not know their names. At the dinner table after they were born, he prayed for them, saying, "please bless these children we're working with." They call my mother Mimi, which was her mother's name, and cry to be passed into her arms from mine. My mother says, "Don't be mad, all children do this." I know that's not true, but I am not mad.

Sometimes, when they are sleeping, I lean into Lars and Maud's cribs and whisper, "Remember who you are."

Acknowledgments

Special thanks to my agent, Emma Patterson, my editor, James Cihlar, and everyone at Howling Bird Press.

I would like to thank Friends of Writers (Larry Levis Post-Graduate Fellowship) and Money for Women (Barbara Deming Memorial Award) for their votes of confidence and generous grants to work on this book. Thank you to the Millay Colony for the Arts for a bucolic setting in which to write. I'll never forget the smell of wild thyme underfoot at the tennis courts, the black bear I encountered in the woods, and the meaningful conversations.

Thank you to the journals who first published some of the stories here—*Epoch* ("Irreversible Things"), *New England Review* ("Lost Things"), *The Collagist* ("Making Sandwiches with My Father"), *Knee-Jerk* ("Glossary"), and *Opium* ("Mother").

Thank you to Lenore Myka, Jennifer Kelly, and Emma Patterson for reading full drafts of this manuscript and helping me turn it into something much better.

Many thanks to my teachers—Karen Brennan, Michael Martone, David Haynes, and Melanie Rae Thon. I'd also like to give a shout-out to my ninth grade creative writing teacher, Ms. Edvalson, who almost made me faint by pulling me out into the hallway one day and telling me that I should never stop writing stories. May we all do something equally meaningful for an incredibly shy and anxious teenager.

Thank you to my Cambridge/Somerville people, my Warren Wilson people, and my Salt Lake City people.

Thank you to my twins, Lars and Maud, for being excellent sleepers while I finished this book. Thank you to my husband, Daniel, the king of extroverts, who didn't take it too personally when I needed alone time. And thank you to my parents and siblings who put up with being made into characters. The characters in this book don't even begin to capture the wit, wisdom, and complexity of their namesakes.

Wooey guysies!

About Lisa Van Orman Hadley

Photo: Niels Jensen

Lisa Van Orman Hadley graduated from the Warren Wilson MFA Program for Writers. She received the Larry Levis Post-Graduate Fellowship, a Barbara Deming Memorial Fund grant, and a Millay Colony fellowship to work on *Irreversible Things*. Her stories have appeared in *Epoch*, *New England Review*, and *The Collagist*.

About Howling Bird Press

Howling Bird Press is the publishing house of Augsburg University's Master of Fine Arts in Creative Writing program. We offer an annual book contest in alternating genres: poetry, fiction, and nonfiction. The contest is open to emerging and established authors, and receives submissions from across the country. The author is awarded a cash prize, book publication, and an invitation to read at the MFA program's summer residency in Minneapolis. Our previous books are *Simples* by KateLynn Hibbard, winner of the 2018 Poetry Prize; *Still Life with Horses* by Jean Harper, winner of the 2017 Nonfiction Prize; *The Topless Widow of Herkimer Street* by Jacob M. Appel, winner of the 2016 Fiction Prize; and *At the Border of Wilshire & Nobody* by Marci Vogel, winner of the 2015 Poetry Prize. Howling Bird Press books are distributed by Small Press Distribution; they are available online and in fine bookstores everywhere.

Howling Bird Press acknowledges our editors Khadijo Abdi, Adin Greenstein, Brad Hagen, and Tracy Ross. The press also thanks MFA Director Stephan Clark, Associate Director Lindsay Starck, Professor Cass Dalglish, Administrative Assistant Kathleen Matthews, and all the faculty, mentors, staff, and students of Augsburg's MFA in Creative Writing. We thank English Department Chair Robert J. Cowgill and Augsburg President Paul Pribbenow. Special thanks to the supporters of the Howling Bird Press Publishing Fund, who—through Augsburg's Give to the Max campaign—provided generous support for this year's project, including James Cihlar, Cass Dalglish, Katherine Fagen, Diana Lopez Jones, Paul Pribbenow, and Thomas D. Redshaw.